The Sidekick Chronicles: Sixx and the Beginning

(Prequel)

Becca Vincenza

Copyright

Books by Becca Vincenza

HEXED SERIES

Hexed Hearts

Hunter's Heart

THE REBIRTH SERIES

Stolen

Damaged

Healed

Burned

Drowned

Tamed

MERCENARIES FOR HIRE

Freelance

Hired

Contracted

Authorized

CURSE BREAKER SERIES

Art of Death

Secrets of the Dead

Dance with Death

THE SIDEKICK CHRONICLES

Sixx and the Hellhound

Sixx and the Fae

Sixx and the Incubus

Sixx Saves the World

Dedication

To my best friend

Note:

This is a prequel novella to the Sidekick Chronicles. Sixx and Ana's story can be started here or in *Sixx and the Hellhound*. This is how Ana and Sixx became friends and how Sixx landed her position as Sidekick extraordinaire.

Sixx and the Hellhound happens years after this prequel.

Preface

If you had said to me, "Sixx, those paranormal creatures from the books you obsessively read are real. Oh, and they're planning on killing you because you're aware of their existence," I would have, well, probably given you a strange look and been done with it, or maybe laughed.

I definitely wouldn't have believed you. I would have hoped that I'd be a heroine who found her mate and turned into this badass, powerful woman. I definitely wouldn't have thought that I'd be covered in grime, blood, sweat, and tears. This had not been the future I envisioned for myself.

At the beginning of the school year, my only thought was of the two more semesters I had to trudge through before I left for college. It wasn't even the appeal of the whole "college experience" for me. It was about getting out of this town, starting a new life.

"Sixx, are you okay?" the voice next to me hissed.

My head bobbed, and I heard it then—the strange cackling sound.

Oh…oh shit, that came from me.

"Just a little bit longer, Sixx. Hold on just a little bit longer."

I laughed to myself. *If only.*

Chapter 1

There is a great misconception that the wallflower in high school *wants* to be noticed. That she *wants* the popular jock, bad boy, whoever the heartthrob is. Some of us want to make it through high school and move on to college.

Life would begin then, or at least, that was what I was led to believe. Who knew? But for now, this small town that I had lived in my entire life, where I had gone to school with almost the same three hundred people, would forget me the day after graduation. That wasn't me belittling myself but the plain, cold truth.

As I sat eating my uninspiring lunch, I tried to focus all of my attention on the book I had brought with me. Unfortunately, there was a bit of a disturbance in the force. Or rather the lunchroom. The new girl who started at the beginning of the year walked in.

She caused a stir, no matter where she went. A big part of it had to do with her California, movie star looks. Her platinum blond hair draped down her shoulders about to her midback, always in beach waves. She was tall and soft enough to make her any guy's dream girl with all the right curves.

Honestly, I didn't give her much thought besides the one class we shared and lunch. If it weren't for the gaggle of girls following her with hate in their eyes and guys catcalling, it'd be a relatively peaceful lunch hour. The other part drawing most of the school's attention was that she hadn't picked a group yet.

As far as I knew, her name was Anastasia, and she didn't talk to many people. She was a loner of the highest degree. Part of me thought about offering a hand of friendship, but she didn't lack options. So, I refocused my attention back on my book.

My heart rate picked up a bit as I hit a rather exciting part of the story. I sat up a little straighter as I rushed through the passage.

Smack.

I jerked as I dropped the book, losing my place, and glared at the offender.

"Sorry, they wouldn't seem to leave me be unless I sat with someone, so I hope you don't mind."

I blinked up at the new girl, "Um…"

"Seriously, why are all small towns the same? At least, in bigger cities, they ignore you and let you be. All of these—oh, can I have one of those? Anyway." She popped a fry into her mouth and sighed. "You all care too much."

"Uh…"

"Oops, well, that's the bell," she said thirty seconds before it rang. I blinked as she stood up and waved at me. "See ya. Thanks for the rescue."

"Huh?"

After she left, I shook my head as I picked up my book and my tray of food. I dumped the remaining lunch that I had neglected into the trash. My mom had commented about my eating habits before I left the house, which stuck with me. Eating didn't hold much appeal to me today, hence my book.

I needed to let the interaction that I had with my mom and Anastasia go. I still had a couple more classes until school was done for the day and I got to go home. Not that it was much of a reprieve from school. My next class would be a breeze, though. After my computer tech class, I'd have math.

Puffing my cheeks out, I headed to my locker. I *hated* math.

My next class flew by. It was one of my favorite classes. Since this new age was so surrounded by technology, my parents pushed me into these classes. It turned out I excelled at it. Most of the time, when the assignments were given to us, I'd finish early and then research other techniques. That class went by like a breeze, but math? I cringed just thinking about it.

Today, I had to run back to my locker before math since I had been so caught up in the strange exchange that I had with the new girl that I forgot to grab my textbook. I walked down the hallway lined with lockers and classrooms spaced between them. The industrial-style tile undertow just added to the blandness of this school.

As I rounded the corner leading down to the hallway that held my locker, two voices filtered through. Almost everyone else had abandoned the hallways since the first warning bell had gone off.

"Look, Boris."

"It's Forrest."

"Okay. Boris, I really don't care what you want. Leave me be."

"It's not Boris," Forrest growled. Forrest, the high school heartthrob who was well out of everyone's league. Forrest, who didn't date – at least, no one from our school. Forrest once offered to give me a mechanical pencil when I didn't have one for a second-grade test.

Slam.

I flinched as a hand smacked the locker.

"I'm giving you a friendly warning."

My stomach sank; I wasn't the hero-complex type. I didn't love the idea of diving into dangerous situations. I liked to believe I was a decent person. But sometimes, just the knowledge of someone else witnessing a situation was enough for bullies to back down.

Taking a deep breath, I stepped around the corner. Forrest stood threateningly over Anastasia, who looked bored. Forrest's nostrils flared, and his narrowed gaze shifted to me.

"Hey, Sixx, aren't you going to be late for class?" he practically snarled.

"Sure am. But you're blocking my locker." I stared pointedly at where his hand slammed into the locker. Was that a...*dent*?

"Boris and I were just finishing up. Sorry to have locker blocked you." Anastasia gave us both a saucy wink before pushing Forrest back. He couldn't mask his shock that she managed to move him. Heck, I was a little surprised, too. He wasn't a small dude, and she wasn't exactly posing for any bodybuilder competitions.

Forrest's top lip peeled back before he shook his head, watching her leave. His hand still pressed on the locker that I claimed was mine. Keeping up the ruse that the locker was mine, I cleared my throat. Yup, I was too chicken shit to walk to my locker and grab my books until he was gone. Forrest looked over at me again.

"See you around, Sixx," Forrest said with a growl in his tone. I had to be reading too many books because teenagers didn't growl. I rolled my eyes at my thoughts and waited until he rounded the corner. My shoulders dropped heavily as I made it the next couple feet away to where my locker was. I ignored the slight dent in the locker door where Forrest had slammed his hand.

I grabbed my book before heading back to my math class. I arrived late, getting the stink-eye from the teacher, who continued with her lesson. While I hated math, the teacher was kind and tried to make it more engaging. We were usually set up into pods of four. Apparently, my pod had taken a drastic change since two seats were empty, and one was filled by someone new.

I slipped into my seat and tried not to stare at Anastasia, who was not in my pod before.

"Sixx, how about you give the equation a try?"

My attention snapped back to the whiteboard and the question of the day, written in black marker, taunting me. I groaned. My heart pounded as more students turned to look back at me. I hated this, hated it. Didn't teachers understand that some people—aka me, for example—absolutely shut down in situations like this? I sank a little lower in my seat. For a split second, regret hit me as I realized this was probably punishment for walking in late. But it had been the right thing to help Ana.

"Actually, Mrs. McGregor, can I?" Anastasia asked, fluttering her lashes. The teacher didn't look impressed but conceded. I breathed a little easier. And just like that, Ana came to my rescue in return.

Anastasia returned to her desk, and I could have sworn I saw the chair move by itself. She didn't touch it, but it had been flush against the desk. I blinked a couple of times before shaking my head. She slipped back into her seat and scooted forward, the legs scraping against the tile.

Nope. I rejected those thoughts. I was just going bananas since the day had been so stressful. And I didn't eat lunch. I nodded to myself. Yup, that was exactly what it was. Stress and low blood sugar.

****

With no more strange events for the rest of the day, which made me feel like I had walked into the Twilight Zone, I headed home. The school was only a couple of miles from my house, shortened if I took the path through the park. It had been the way I used since I had started second grade. My parents often forgot to pick me up. And due to my lack of desire to sit on a bus for twice the amount of time it took to walk, I skipped the bus.

It also made my mother quite excited to think that I was managing to get a daily workout in; unfortunately, my massive number of curves was due to genetics, not overeating. Maybe a little overeating. And I decided long ago not to walk every single day. I'd catch the bus or a friend would take me home, especially during winter.

The pathway I took had transformed into my favorite season. Summer had released its death grip, and fall came barreling in. Rustic reds, burnt oranges, and vibrant yellows arched over me. I sighed heavily, taking in that fall scent. Fallen leaves with the crisp scent of the edge of winter. I tucked my hands further into my pockets. This walk helped soothe my nerves concerning any school problems, but today I kept replaying my interactions with Anastasia.

She didn't seem unkind, and she had a more outgoing personality than I did. So then, why wasn't she gravitating to a group? Any group? I shook my head. It was not my concern and certainly not my problem. As I broke through the park on the other side, I entered the subdivision that held my house. Or rather, my parents' house.

It would be much easier to slip between houses to get to the oh-so-clever and not at all generic street name— Peach Avenue. But Apple, Tangerine, and Rose Streets mostly housed homes that had dogs. And those dogs needed fences. And even those without dogs had privacy fences. So I walked around the subdivision to get home.

Each house was designed and built from a model. Each house had a Stepford Wives, creepy, similar look. Even as I walked down the street, I had a hard time deciphering the differences.

I strolled into a parking lot with landscaping that matched everyone else's on this lane, not because of an insane HOA but because my parents preferred to match those around them. The windows were dark, and no cars sat in the driveway. I sighed heavily as I walked up to the door.

I tried twisting the knob; unsurprisingly, it was locked. I dug through my backpack and pulled out my house keys before flipping the lock over and stepping into the empty, dark house.

"Home sweet home," I muttered, my voice dropping on deaf ears. Just me again tonight.

Chapter 2

The next week followed the same routine. Not that my life usually strayed too far from the normal. The only difference now was that Anastasia stopped to eat lunch with me at least twice this week. The more popular girls who wanted to absorb her into their group did not take kindly to it. They liked knowing the status quo, and having her as an anomaly freaked them out. And because she had decided to show an interest in me, they set their eyes on me.

Ah, to be considered part of the décor again. I rolled my eyes at the thought as I pushed my glasses up the bridge of my nose, keeping my head down during math class. The rest of our pod returned the day after. The teacher rearranged us a bit, but Anastasia and I shared it with Ashley A. and Nicole. The two girls wanted Anastasia where they could keep their eye on her.

"So, Seven."

"It's Sixx." I paused, muttering the next part under my breath. "You've known me since first grade." I kept my head down as I worked on the worksheet we were given.

"Yeah, whatever, Five. We heard that your parents are usually gone, leaving you all alone in that big ol' house of yours. Would you consider throwing a welcoming party for your new friend Anastasia here?" Nicole patted Anastasia, who gave her the stink eye. I almost snorted but stifled it.

My brows pinched as my face twisted into distaste at the idea of a party. Ashley A., though, narrowed her gaze on me. Her lips spread into a devious smile that made me uncomfortable.

"Aren't you two close?" Ashley A. asked, her tone implying something more.

Sighing heavily, I looked up from my work. My instincts knew the best way to deal with her was to ignore her. And as much as I wanted her comments not to bother me, I didn't like what she was asking. "Why is that your business? And I don't know why you would think that."

Because really, we weren't what I would call...*close.*

"Forrest said you two have been eating lunch practically every day together," Nicole said with a bit of a sneer. I sucked in a breath, my eyes widening a bit.

"This is none of your business, but since you two are so interested in my and *Sixx's* relationship, she has been tutoring me in math."

I made a choked noise.

Both Queen Bee types looked at each other before bursting into laughter.

"Little Five over here was named after a number because she is so bad with them. Her parents had hoped that it would help with her grades," Nicole said, still laughing a little. Anastasia looked at me and shrugged. My cheeks burned. It wasn't a secret that I burst into tears in first grade during a math test because I had been so frustrated with some of the more basic math questions. It probably wouldn't have been something that most people remembered. Besides, Nicole pointed out that I should know numbers since my name was one. The class cracked up.

That moment didn't mold me into a math geek. Instead, I shied from it and often struggled to keep my math grades up. It wasn't a secret that I asked for extra credit.

"Yeah, you're not wrong. Math is not my strong suit," I agreed, hoping that if I did, they would leave me be. I didn't even care about their unclever nicknames for me. Calling me by a different number didn't hurt my feelings like they were hoping it would. Most people didn't know the real reason behind my name. When I asked my mom when I was turning six, she had been stressed with work and forgot the fake story they had told me.

My mother had the type of pregnancy where she didn't realize I existed until well into her third trimester. Rare, but not unheard of. My parents were wholly unprepared for a child. A child, they both decided long before they got married, that they didn't want. They both vehemently ignored the bun burning in the oven until the night of my birth—June 6th, at six a.m. My parents couldn't have thought of a more original name like Lilith or something. Nope, they went straight for the kill. Sixx.

That isn't to say my parents weren't smart because they were. My father was a college professor, and my mother worked for multiple charities and in the corporate world for a long time. But with kids? They had no idea. If it hadn't been for pressure from my father's mom, I don't know if they would have kept me. Even if they had the means financially, they moved to the 'burbs, and my grandmother lived with us for the first couple of years of my life, taking care of me until she passed away.

"Anyway, since Five won't have you, come to Forrest's dad's cabin this weekend with us, Anastasia. Going to be a full moon. That is when we all can get a little beastly," Nicole said with an implied tone, for which I didn't understand the reference. But then again, I stayed away from the typical high school scene.

I refocused my attention back on my work.

"Yeah, no thanks. I prefer not to see a bunch of hairy asses in the middle of the night running through the woods," Anastasia said.

What the hell did high schoolers do nowadays?

Tension crackled in the air as both of them went silent. I peeked up through my lashes to see Anastasia and Nicole having a stare-off. I shifted in my seat, uncomfortable. My stomach dropped as a part of me screamed to leave. *Run.* Anxiety crackled under my skin like ants crawling all over me. I wanted *out.*

"Tone it down, Nicole," Ashley A. hissed. My eyes narrowed when she quite obviously jerked her chin in my direction. Anastasia slammed her hand down, and I could have sworn I saw blue electricity crackling between her knuckles. But that was insanity. I blinked, convincing myself it was static electricity. My anxiety spiked again, and the marching ants turned into millions of centipedes with thousands of legs. I wanted *out* of this seat, immediately.

"Stop, you bitch. Or I will stop you myself," Anastasia snapped.

The tension broke, fracturing like a bone. My lungs deflated as I was finally able to release a long breath. The three girls in our pod looked at me. Anastasia smiled, Nicole gave me a disgusted look, and Ashley A. gave me side-eye.

Even Ashley W., a pod over, gave me a look.

"I think I need to go to the bathroom," I muttered before standing to speak with the teacher. She agreed with a quick nod, and I headed to the bathroom.

Once I arrived, I stood in front of the porcelain white sink and the dirty mirror. I shook my head at myself, trying to clear my thoughts. My anxiety finally settled, but it still tightened my stomach. Was I getting a cold? Maybe it had just been some weird chills that I got.

I'd see if my friend Caroline could take me home in her car for the rest of the week. During the summers, I worked at a small mom and pop shop with some minimal groceries and an ice cream bar. My parents probably wouldn't care one way or the other if I worked through the school year, but I wanted to focus on getting decent grades. After two summers, I still hadn't saved up enough to get a car, but hopefully, before I left for college, I would.

There was a good chance that my parents would get me one if I asked, but I learned after my grandmother passed that I needed to support myself. My parents would help but in their own way.

After splashing a bit of water on my face, my thoughts cleared. It was getting colder outside, so it would make sense that I might be on the verge of a cold. Nodding once to myself, I headed back to class, feeling much better.

****

Other than the strange event in math, the rest of my week played out as it normally did. Caroline agreed to drive me to and from school, which I appreciated, knowing that it was a little bit out of her way. But she always enjoyed the company; she and I had known each other forever. She had grand plans after high school, too. She wanted to leave and go to Los Angeles.

That was mostly her plan, and then she would figure it out from there. It had been her dream for as long as I had known her.

"Friday night, you got big plans, Sixx?"

"Oh yeah, you know me," I muttered, pressing my head against her car window. The week had been long, and I was ready for the weekend. A whole weekend while my parents were away—that was a lucky guess on Nicole's part. But it meant a full weekend when I could read or watch my "ridiculous" shows. My mother didn't care much for my choice in, well, anything. While he could get on board with some classics like *Star Trek*, my father drew the line at my cult classics. Sometimes it just soothed the soul.

Caroline laughed.

"Well, I'll let you know if something saucier comes up than your...novels," she said, wiggling her eyebrows at me, poking me in the side. I laughed. She and our other friend would probably end up making a mall trip. Unless they ended up at the bookstore, I'd remain behind.

"All right, you don't have too much fun this weekend, Sixx," Caroline said with a wave. I climbed out of the car and waved to her.

I headed into the dark house once again. Loneliness hit me hard as I stepped inside. Even though I had been with Caroline only moments before, stepping into this empty house hit me harder on some days than others. And despite Caroline inviting me along with her and the other girls, all of whom I'd known for a very long time, sometimes I felt like an outsider. Even if my parents were home, I'd still feel the pang that I felt now.

Breathing in, I dragged my bag upstairs to my room. The house was still in the model form of the rest of the houses on the block. The living room was blocked off by a small dining room, which connected to the kitchen. And the den where my father had his office and a half bathroom was on the first level. Upstairs housed my room, their master, and a guest room that doubled as my mother's office. There was a bathroom that I used and the master bedroom.

As I entered my room, I flopped on the bed and considered messaging Caroline back to see how far she'd made it. But I discarded that idea. I should spend the evening getting my homework done now so I wouldn't leave it for the last minute. Some people worked great under pressure; some people spent all weekend stressing about not getting their work done. I was definitely the latter.

I set myself up on my bed with my laptop and started to work through my homework. After a couple of hours, I stretched my back out, climbing off the bed. Homework completed, I got to treat myself with a book and food.

Going to the kitchen, I opened the fridge and the cabinets, but there was nothing to make. I guess it would be delivery tonight. I pulled my phone out of my back pocket, ordered food, and then switched over to my Kindle app. It'd be a quiet night for me.

Chapter 3

Aawhooo.

I shivered. Unfortunately, not from the chill of the night air. This was not the first, not even the second or third, but about the fifth wolf cry. Why I decided I needed to go for a walk to get out of my head, I didn't know.

Friday night, I had stayed in, eaten my dinner, and read a book. Earlier today, I occupied myself with a bit more outside studies of computer sciences and looking into colleges that would be the best options for my career choice. I wanted something that would revolve around research and a bit of discovery. My major decision was miles and miles away.

But the later the night got, the lonelier and darker the house became. My parents would be returning sometime tomorrow, which left me alone for the rest of the night. I thought maybe a stroll would help. But then I remembered what Nicole said about it being a full moon. I shivered, pulling my oversized sweater closer to my body.

I huffed, my rounded cheeks blistered by the cold chill in the night air. I kept expecting a wolf to pop out from between the trees. I had made it to the park that I walked through to get to school and back. I hadn't realized how far I'd walked while I listened to my music. I had been caught up in the songs and mindless scrolling through my social media that I pulled my headphones down when I looked up.

That had been about ten minutes ago, and I could still hear the echoing sounds of the wilderness around us. We lived in a populated area, and I didn't think animals would come too close, but the sound was getting closer.

My heart rate kicked up as panic started to squeeze at my chest. I twisted around, deciding it was high time to return home. As I spun on my heel, a blurred shape appeared then flashed out of my sight. Jerking my attention back to the trimmed garden, I almost laughed at myself— just a statue. Breathing out, I turned my attention back to the path.

My heart jumped into my throat, and I couldn't breathe. My eyes widened as I instinctively took a step back—the wrong move.

A beast stood in front of me. There was no way it was an actual wolf. Not that I had seen a wolf in real life or any closer than a zoo trip back in eighth grade. But the monster in front of me…was like dire-wolf–sized. Even those CGI wolves looked weak compared to this beast. Muscle bunched under matted, dirty fur. Yellowed teeth were on sharp display as drool dripped down its jowls.

A chest-rattling growl rolled from the beast, making me whimper.

Pinned ears, sharp yellow eyes, and dangerous claws completed the midnight wolf's intimidation. The wolf's shoulders stood at about the same height as mine, and hell, I wasn't tall by any means, but a wolf shouldn't be that big!

Oh my fucking God. Oh my fucking…God.

I took another step back, and the wolf dropped its head a little further between its shoulders, watching me. It bared its front teeth at me as it flicked its tongue out to lick its top lip and nose.

If I didn't already doubt the existence of this entirely too large wolf, the hint of excitement that flooded its eyes proved it to me. This creature was unnatural. My back tensed, and my muscles burned for me to move, run until I was out of breath and couldn't go any farther.

My breathing became erratic because even if I ran, I was pretty sure the wolf's legs were longer than mine. Not to mention that it had two extra ones. It would walk and still keep up with me.

"This is not how I wanted to die," I whimpered. Not that I spent a lot of afternoons contemplating my death, but it was something we all thought about at least once. I had hoped that I would make it at least past my thirties. I mean, the goal had been my late eighties or nineties.

The wolf growled, regaining all my attention again. Its shoulder blades loosened a little. I didn't like what that implied at all. At. All.

Blind panic took over, and I bolted. I didn't even know what direction I went, but my brain misfired when I realized the beast was playing with me at this point. It could have leaped and attacked. Why it was even here made no sense. Not that I had a lot of knowledge about wolves, other than werewolves from the fiction novels I read. I didn't think real wolves liked to be around humans. And I thought they would only attack if they felt provoked.

But where did this beast even come from? An excited yip came from behind me. I wanted to say it was almost cute, save for the fact it was chasing me down to eat me, so...not cute.

My glasses bounced dangerously on my face; they were too loose, and I needed to get them tightened. I had needed to get it done for weeks, but I had been putting it off. As I tripped, they flew off my face into the darkness of the park.

"Fuck," I hissed.

The crashing of manicured bushes and trees sounded right next to me. I yelped as moist, hot breaths puffed against my cheek. When a droplet of saliva dripped down my arm, leaving a slimy trail, I almost passed out. But my heart pushed the adrenaline faster through my body, encouraging me to continue to live and move my ass.

My hands dug into the ground underneath me. Spontaneous planning was not my forte, but right now, my body reacted to instincts. The most basic survival instincts. Fight or flight. Flight was my only option.

I dropped to the ground and rolled away from the beast, hoping the move would confuse it. At this point, I did not doubt that the creature was messing with me. The wolf made a snarly bark sound before powering through the bushes after me again. Teeth snapped right beside my ear, and this time, I couldn't hold back my bloodcurdling scream.

My throat felt hoarse as I scrambled to my feet. I searched the blurry ground for some sort of weapon. Anything to keep him away. My scream should have been able to draw attention, right?

I backed up a step as the beast came into my range of view. It looked practically gleeful, its lips upturned, and it was dipped low as if it was going to launch itself.

My back hit the sharp, unforgiving bark of a healthy oak. I didn't dare take my eyes off the animal in front of me. I was panting short, staggered breaths, and the world went dizzy around me. Sweat pooled behind my neck as frustrated tears prickled in my eyes.

This really hadn't been my plan. I didn't want to be dinner for a creature that shouldn't exist. It had to be a radioactive mutant wolf.

In my books, even in TV shows or movies, the damsel in distress looked away as death sprang forward to rip out her throat, but I couldn't seem to take my eyes off the beast. Its hind legs bunched, and its tail flickered once as it let out a bloodcurdling roar.

And my heart stopped.

A blue streak of crackling electricity shot between the wolf and me. It ran right into it, its fur singed, and the smell of burned hair reached my nose.

"Damn, I'm glad that worked," a familiar voice said. My heart picked up its racing speed again. My stomach twisted as my knees threatened to buckle underneath me.

"Hey, Sixx," Anastasia said as she stepped farther into the space. She threw her hand out, and a gust of wind knocked into me. I collapsed, my palms scraping against the harsh underbrush. The wolf turned its attention to Ana and peeled back its lips.

"Oooh, you are one ugly bitch," Anastasia taunted as she remained utterly unaffected by the raging winds that whipped around the wolf and me. Leaves and loose branches smacked against the wolf as I threw my arms over the back of my head to try to protect my neck.

"Okay," Anastasia said as she shook out her arms, and the wind started to slow down. The wolf mostly looked more pissed than it had previously been. Anastasia breathed in before opening her eyes, and blue electric currents sparked and crackled between her fingertips.

"Let's play," she taunted with a crazy-ass smile. How was she making lightning bolts sprout between her fingers? How was any of this happening? My mind raced, but I needed to focus on something. My mind laser-focused on the wolf. Its attention went back to Anastasia, who rushed forward, looking small compared to the massive beast. But she had a bold look on her face as she threw her fist backward and flung it forward into its jaw.

The wolf surprisingly stumbled backward as she landed her punch. Anastasia whooped before backing off.

"Sorry, Sixx. I didn't bring any weapons; otherwise, I would hand one to you. I just happened to be out on a run," she said, bouncing in place. She wore spandex-like leggings with mesh netting for a pocket on the leg and a tight tank top. Her pale, milky skin shone under the moonlight, her hair, which was in a tight ponytail, bouncing as she moved.

"Weapons?" I muttered, still blinking at her, not understanding anything.

"Hang on," Anastasia said as she whipped her leg out in a roundhouse kick that I was certain only happened in old martial arts movies. Anastasia's sparkling blue electricity spread up her arms. The wolf lunged forward, its teeth on full display. Ana attacked.

She moved like she was well-trained and knew exactly what to do in this situation. But I mean, at the same time, of course, she did. She had blue magic. My head spun wildly at that. The wolf snarled and realized that Ana would be too much of a threat. It turned its attention back to me. I screamed as it lurched forward.

I lifted my arm to protect my face, and its teeth sank into my shoulder.

The pain was blinding. It took my breath away. My brain reacted violently, wanting the pain to stop, so I started to shake and pull away. The wolf continued to tear at my shoulder.

"Sixx, stop!" Anastasia yelled at me. It was next to impossible, but I calmed enough for Anastasia to rush forward. She slammed her hands over the beast's eyes. It roared, releasing its hold on me. I breathed heavily, feeling lightheaded.

The scent of burning fur hit me again. Bile crawled up my throat as my stomach heaved. Anastasia landed a kick to the wolf's side that sent it reeling. The wolf bared its teeth at Anastasia once again. Its nostrils flared as it blindly looked in the small area where they had been battling. Squinting, I noticed burned fur around the wolf's eyes, and wetness flowed from them.

My features pinched up in disgust. I could barely handle seeing gore on TV but seeing it in real life? Combined with the coppery scent of its blood, I barely kept from throwing up.

The loss of blood from the good chunk he got from my arm made me feel even dizzier. Anastasia rushed to my side.

"Oh, shit. Okay. I've done this for my aunt like a hundred times. Okay, trust me."

"I'm doubting you for the number of times you said okay," I mumbled, listing to the side.

"Oh no, don't do that," she whispered as she grabbed my uninjured arm.

"The wolf," I muttered.

Anastasia looked over her shoulder at the beast, who pawed at its right eye. But as it got more irate, it turned its attention back to us. Blood rushed down the wolf's face as it paced forward.

"Anastasia!"

"Seriously, Sixx, you can call me Ana."

"Not the time!" I yelled, pointing at the beast that moved closer to us. Ana sighed and looked over her shoulder.

"If you don't go back to your pack, asshole, I will destroy you."

Oh God. There were more of them? Was that what she meant by pack?

It lunged forward, eyeing my leg. I pulled it back, accidentally knocking Ana over. I didn't realize she was holding a concrete swirling ball of fire and her crackling electricity. Ana's eyes went wide as she lost her concentration. The magic splintered with a cracking sound, exploding out of her control. The force of the exploding magic knocked my head against the tree behind me. My vision went black.

Chapter 4

My back ached something fierce; when I rolled over, my muscles screamed. I peeked an eye open only to be greeted with dirt. The night's events hit me over the head, and I jerked upright, squinting to understand the world around me. The earth had been disturbed by the battle between a seemingly magical girl and a massive wolf. But that was insane.

That was insane.

All of it.

I stood, but my knees were weak. Hell, I felt helpless in general. I gripped the tree behind me. Ana and the wolf were both gone. The city-maintained bushes and flowers were trampled, and branches were snapped in half. There was no way that something didn't happen.

But maybe people visiting the park with their dogs had trampled them. I touched my shoulder where it should have been mangled, but I was greeted with torn fabric. That sucked because it was one of my favorite shirts. A few pinprick size spots on the skin under the torn fabric looked a little like scars.

My head spun as it tried to land on a logical reason for all this.

Bug bites. I nodded to myself. Yes, that's what it was.

"Yup. All right, time to get up, Sixx," I said to myself as I got my knees underneath me again. I used the tree to help me up and searched the surrounding area for my glasses. Thankfully, after squinting too hard, I found them a couple of yards away.

I felt gritty, sweaty, and just dirty after somehow falling asleep out here. I stumbled through the park on my way home.

****

My dad's car, which they took with them on their mini-vacation getaway, was in the driveway. I walked into the house. The foyer was clear of their shoes, my mom's purse, and their coats.

"Sixx! You're filthy! Get out of the doorway, and go shower before you leave a whole trail behind you," my mother exclaimed as she came from the kitchen into the living room with two coffee mugs. My father sat up a little straighter on the couch and looked over at me. I blinked hard because, after my night in the park, that was all she had to say. But she didn't know what had happened. Hell, I didn't know what happened.

"Hmm." And his attention returned to his documentary. I ducked my head and ran up the stairs. They probably assumed that I went out for a walk and tripped. I usually wasn't exceptionally clumsy, but I had my moments. I'd go with that, too.

I headed upstairs to the bathroom and took a quick shower. I refused to think about the night that I had. Because it had been leftovers from my reading combined with my overactive imagination, I must have been exhausted while I was on my walk and stopped for a break.

All of it, all of my excuses, made me feel better, even though in the back of my head, I knew something wasn't right. I knew it. I stepped out of the shower and wrapped a towel around my body. My phone had died, not surprising since I probably left my music app going throughout the night. I snagged it and bundled up my dirty clothes.

Once I got into my room, I dropped my clothes into my laundry basket filled with clothes I would need to wash today. But my head still ached, and the nightmare that felt far too vivid still lingered in my mind. I put on some comfy clothes and snuggled onto my bed.

I had truly only meant to take a little nap. When I woke up three hours later, I began to rush around the house. My parents were on the couch, still watching their shows. My mom was working on her laptop. But neither asked me about my weekend, just let me get my work done.

After three loads of laundry—not all my clothes—and taking out the trash into the garage, it was time to start thinking about dinner. My dad stepped into the kitchen and asked if I wanted to help him. Since we spent so little time together, I agreed, not to mention that it would keep my mind off everything.

Dinner had been pleasant. My parents told me how they met up with another couple they had known back in their college days. They did a bit of golfing, and they had an enjoyable dinner. My mother mentioned how it had been nice to neglect work for a day. I smiled because even though they put a lot of stock in me taking care of myself, I knew they both worked hard.

"Sixx, what did you get up to this weekend? No crazy house parties, right?" my dad joked.

"Nope, just some crazy homework. Then I went for a walk in the park."

"Yes, we saw the dirt trail," my mom said with a fragile smile that didn't reach her eyes. I swallowed down my retort to tell her that I spent my time out in the park. It wouldn't do any good to worry about them. If anything, she would want me to go to the doctor to make sure that I didn't get bitten by something larger than the bugs outside.

I paled at the thought, remembering those yellowed teeth and the drool that dripped down the wolf's muzzle. I shook my head. It was a nightmare.

After dinner, my parents cleaned up, moving over the sink as they spoke to each other. My father was a robust man and my mother petite. But it was evident that they loved each other. Smiling at the sight of them and reassuring myself that they were home with me tonight, I headed back upstairs.

My phone was still on the charger, powered down and completely forgotten.

****

The next morning, surprisingly, I was still so tired that I slept through my first alarm. If it hadn't been for my mom swinging into my room, I would have been extremely late for school. I grabbed my phone at the last minute and caught a ride with my dad to school. I ran inside as the first warning bell went off. I breathed a little easier as I headed to my locker. And to my complete disappointment, Ana was leaning against it. My stomach dropped.

It was a dream.

A. Dream.

Ana looked up from her phone as relief crossed her features.

"Sixx! Why haven't you answered your phone?"

My eyebrows bunched together with confusion. I pulled out my phone, and it was still powered off, so I turned it on. As soon as it went through all the displays, I saw I'd missed almost a hundred messages. I looked up at Ana.

She just shrugged her shoulder at me. Then, my phone started to vibrate in my hand, and I had twenty-seven new text messages.

"Jeez."

"I thought our *friend* came back. I couldn't find you," Ana hissed as she stepped a little closer. Her shoulders were tense, and her eyes were filled with concern.

"What do you mean, our friend? Also, how did you have my phone number?"

"Okay, tell me right now that when I," Ana leaned closer, "healed you, I didn't fuck up your memories?"

The blood drained from my head so quickly that I thought I was going to faint.

"That...what happened in the park was a dream," I said, slightly hysterical.

"Sixx, calm down. I know it's a lot to take in. Hence why I tried to contact you. I came back for you when I made sure that our *friend*," Ana winked, "left the area."

My heart pounded in my chest. *No, no. No.*

"Sixx, stop screaming no."

Was I screaming?

"You are. And I need you to calm down," Ana said, looking over my shoulder then her own.

"Did I say that out loud?" I asked, my voice raising an octave, which made me think of a scene from a classic sitcom that made me want to burst out into hysterics.

"Sixx." Ana grabbed my face and forced me to lock eyes with her. Jeez, I never realized how blue they were until now. And they seemed to have specks of gold in them. An artificial calm swept over me. "Look, we need to get through this school day as if nothing happened. I promise I will explain things as best I can after. But promise me you won't speak a *word* of what happened on Saturday."

I nodded. Because first off, who would believe me? I didn't believe me.

"Promise me," Ana repeated, tightening her hold on my shoulder where she dropped her hands from my face.

"I promise."

"Good. Okay, I'll see you at lunch," Ana said with a carefree smile that countered the vibe she had been giving me not five seconds before. I blinked, but by the time I got my head on straight, she was gone.

My head spun in circles as I made my way to my first class. I spent the first half of the day writing out lists, questions, setting out plans for when Ana and I could speak freely. About, well, everything. I drifted through my classes without really paying any attention, and it would bite me in the ass later.

I walked out of my class before lunch a little later than I had intended because I was caught up in getting together my most crucial questions. On my way through the school hallways, it started to thin out as more students headed to their next class or lunch.

Raised, annoyed voices caught my attention as I got closer to the lunchroom.

"It was her funky-ass scent again, Forrest."

"Nicole, this is not the place to have this conversation. Just because you don't like her scent doesn't mean it was her."

"I know it was! She knows, and she is keeping shit from us."

"We will talk about this with the...when we get home." He hissed a word that I couldn't hear. I clutched my notebook closer to my chest as I stopped walking and strained to hear how Nicole would respond. They were all in the same circle, so maybe they were talking about the party they were trying to get Ana to go to this weekend?

"The pack doesn't care as long as..."

"Nicole, shut the fuck up." Forrest's voice got deeper than I'd ever heard a high schooler's go, and fear skittered down my spine.

Did she say pack?

"Hey, Sixx!" my friend Caroline called to me as she came out of the office kiddie corner to where the other two were speaking. My heart stopped as I expected them to round the corner and pounce on me.

"Oh, God. Were you headed toward the nurse? If not, you should. You are really pale," Caroline said with a small smile as she touched my elbow. "Do you want me to walk you there? I have a teacher aid hour. I'm sure Mrs. McGregor wouldn't mind if I'm a little late."

I shook my head, trying to swallow even though my mouth was dry.

"I'm here!" Ana said, appearing out of nowhere from behind us. Caroline looked at her then to me.

"You two..."

"Just recently became friends. Sixx graciously let me sit with her during lunch. The least I could do is take her to the nurse."

"Oh, okay. Well, feel better, Sixx," Caroline said with a wave. Ana's smile remained in place until she was gone.

"So, want to get lunch at the small café in town?"

"We aren't allowed off-campus."

"Pfft, we aren't asking, silly. Come on," Ana said with a genuine smile as she pulled me toward the school's closest side entrance. I didn't stop her because suddenly, the school didn't feel like a safe place to have the talk we *needed* to have.

Chapter 5

Anxiety twisted my stomach. This was a normal, natural thing that I witnessed countless students do over the last three and a half years. It was fine. Only, I didn't skip school. Even if we planned on coming back. Ana seemed unfazed as she tugged me up the small sidewalk that led downtown. Little shops were connected in small plazas, each storefront unique but offering a very small-town feel, even if a couple of miles down were fast-food restaurants and big-box stores.

"Look, if they didn't want students to boost the economy during their lunch hour, why else would they place so many better food options close to the school?" Ana argued as she trudged along. I'd say this about her: she seemed very carefree. Lighthearted and unworried about not only what we were doing but what hadn't happened over the weekend.

"Probably it's just a central location, and they were hoping people would pick their kids up from school and come down to get dinner," I muttered, still unnerved as I worked through the events that happened on Saturday night.

"You are smart. I don't know why you said you weren't in math," Ana said with a wink. She slowed her steps, realizing that her normal stride equaled, like, five of mine. Linking her arm with mine, she kept pace with me.

"Because I don't like math, and math doesn't like me. How are you not freaking out right now?" I yelled, staring at her. Did she, this slip of a girl, really beat up a massive dire wolf?

"Why would *I* be freaking out? My life didn't just get knocked off its axis only for me to act like it was one big ol' hallucination."

"Because I know your secret now?" I offered, my voice still a little—okay, a lot—shrill.

"Oh, that's easy. I'll just kill you."

Dizziness swept over me as I staggered forward.

"Kid-ding! Kinda." Ana winked. "Oh jeez, sorry, I'm kidding," she tacked on when she watched me visibly change colors.

"Anyone ever tell you that you have a sick sense of humor?"

Ana shrugged.

"My aunt. We move a lot, so I don't make friends quickly or easily. Or ever, really. Usually for the best since they can't know my secret. And truthfully, a lot of those superhero shows make it more dramatic than it is. Do you know how many people have skeletons in their closets that no one knows about?"

As she spoke, my head spun and spun.

"You...just said a lot."

"I did. You have anything to add?" she asked with a sweet-as-pie smile.

"Maybe?"

"Sorry, I know I can be a lot. Especially when you first met me, well, you know what I mean."

I guessed I did. Because before now, the most we had exchanged were brief conversations. And as I thought over those few interactions, she had never been unkind. If anything, she had been a bit distant. A hit of loneliness spiked when I recalled what she had motor-mouthed at me. That she didn't make friends quickly or easily. It was her and her aunt.

"So, what happened on Saturday..." I hedged toward the real elephant in the room.

"Yeah. About that," Ana said. Her features became a little more shielded; her voice took a different edge. "Sixx, I think it goes without saying, but this needs to stay between us."

"Okay, but will you explain to me what happened?"

Ana got quiet as we got closer to the café in town. We walked in and each ordered something to go. With her warning hanging between us, we remained silent while inside the cafe. We grabbed our food and headed back outside.

We both got wraps, making it easier to eat as we walked. Ana devoured hers before we even made it halfway back to the school.

"What exactly was that beast on Saturday?" I asked since she didn't seem inclined to start the conversation.

Ana gave me a sideways glance before she pursed her lips.

"My aunt warned me to give you the basics. It would be best if you kept all of it to yourself. It'd be better if you forgot it completely, honestly. If you want to go on believing it's a nightmare, that would be best. But I think you deserve a bit of an explanation."

I considered that. It would undoubtedly be the easiest route. And I planned to leave this place once I graduated. Was it any of my concern? But then, my mind worked over everything. Ana had brought me out here. She prompted me to talk about it and offered me tidbits. She had a reason for that.

"We have the rest of the year together. At the very least, I can pretend none of this happened after I leave for college," I offered. Because, in truth, that had been my intention. This would be my last hurrah before college, especially since I didn't plan on sticking around.

"You're an interesting human, Sixx."

I shivered at her calling me human. She laughed at my reaction.

"That makes you not human?"

"Ehh, ish."

"Ish?"

"Yeah, I have some human in me. At least that is what my aunt says. She is my mother's blood sister."

"What happened to your mother, if you don't mind me asking?"

Ana got quiet as we stepped onto school grounds.

"Look, trust me when I say this. Aunt Lola is my only family. It's been her and me for as long as I can remember and probably even before that. Don't give me that look. I probably would have called my aunt Lola 'Mom,' but she made sure to try to keep my mother's spirit alive."

I nodded. That was a pain that I couldn't truly understand. From the little I knew of her, I knew that her life was much different from the one I lived. Remaining quiet, I waited for Ana to speak again.

"Saturday night, that was a werewolf. I am not sure what it was doing in the park. I really can't go into details yet. But I promise that the wolf will not be bothering you again. How's the shoulder doing?" Ana asked. I touched it, thinking about the pain that had been so overwhelming that I knew it couldn't have been a dream.

"It...the...wolf...werewolf bit me," I said, my breathing becoming more erratic. Most of the lore I had read claimed that come next full moon, I'd...oh God.

"Don't worry about turning into one. That is a movie thing. To become one, you need to be born into it. Or have some serious magical intervention."

I looked at her pointedly.

"I just healed you. Well, the best that I could. Aunt Lola told me not to do it often because it leaves a magical signature. Which could lead other paras to me, and we're trying to avoid that."

My mind kept firing new information at me. New questions popped into my head. And the closer we got to the side entrance, the more I realized my time for questions would come to an end. I would need to get some paper and a pen. I had a lot that I needed to write down.

"How about this weekend we get together, and I'll try to fill you in on what I can? I didn't plan this very well, and honestly, I didn't think you would speak with me. I thought you were avoiding me over the weekend," Ana said with a shrug.

If my phone hadn't been turned off, I probably would have ignored most of the many, many phone calls and texts from her. Part of me still wanted to hide my head in the sand and pretend all of this was a dream. But another side of me—that I wished I was better at smothering—was curious. The saying wasn't "curiosity left the cat living a full, healthy life" after all.

"Sounds good to me," I agreed. It probably would be better. It would give me time to think everything through and get my thoughts down on paper.

"Relax, Sixx. I promise it's not as bad as it all sounds," Ana said with an easygoing smile. I didn't feel the same; my anxiety kept crawling upwards. She pulled the door open but leaned forward and looked both ways.

"Coast is clear. In you go," she said, stepping back. I went in first, and Ana quickly followed.

"I'll see you later in math." And she took off.

My world had been turned upside down and inside out, and she expected me to focus on math?

"Okay, super simple," I mumbled.

****

Half the week went by in the same pattern. Ana and I had lunch together, but our conversations were about safe topics. I was brimming with questions, though. Different interactions ran through my mind. The conversation that I overheard between Forrest and Ana didn't go over my head. Nor did the talk between him and Nicole. I just couldn't ask Ana about it. Not yet. *This weekend,* I reminded myself.

Only, that was until Thursday hit. I had been writing down any question that popped into my head so that I wouldn't forget. Plus, when we finally sat down to talk, I knew my mind would blank out. And because I couldn't just sit on my butt, waiting for her to give me answers, I started to do a bit of my own research.

Shifting out any fiction novels, I went to the computer and tried to find the lore that authors might have taken from that might have a grain of truth in them. Mostly since the only thing I had to go off of was werewolves, that was where I focused my research.

The internet went to weird places. I found deeper sites that made me want to cringe, but I looked anyway. They claimed to be hunters of the beasts. The group that I had been researching struck me as imposters. They claimed that silver bullets would kill werewolves and that wolfsbane would weaken them.

It sounded like things from fiction novels that I read and that people who knew anything about the paranormal would know anyway. But I printed off the information, adding it to the notebook that I kept with all the things I wanted to ask Ana about.

I walked out of my computer class, not watching where I was going. I collided with Nicole, who practically growled at me while all my stuff went flying. Groaning, I apologized and dropped down to grab my stuff.

"Watch where you are going, Five," she sneered. I rolled my eyes but collected the papers on the Vycn group that claimed to be werewolf hunters. She stepped over my stuff without giving me a second look. I breathed a little easier.

Walking into my math class, I sat at my pod and pulled out my notebook, intending to put things back into order. But as I opened it up, my back muscles tensed, and my heart rate went up.

"Shit. Shit. Shit," I hissed as I continued to comb through the papers. My first sheet that had initial questions was missing, along with the printout of the Vycn group's seal. Where had they gone? I could have sworn that I packed everything up from the hallway. I stood, ready to go double check when Ana flopped down in her seat.

My nerves pinched with stress. I bit my lip and considered telling Ana. Maybe we would be able to check before class started. But she looked exhausted. Dark circles bloomed under her eyes, and she dropped her forehead on the desk.

"What happened?" I asked, my mind immediately going to the possibility that the werewolf had returned from the other night.

"My aunt ran me through some intense drills last night. I'm still tired. Hey, we still good for this weekend?" she asked with a bit of hope in her voice.

"Yeah." The unease still lingered.

Chapter 6

My heart was hammering away in my chest as my palms grew slick. I clutched my book closer to my chest as I took a step back. Every instinct in me told me to submit and avoid eye contact. Why was he here? Why was he crowding me? My eyes flickered to the cords of muscles in his neck that shouldn't belong to someone my age, yet there he was. I understood the draw of Forrest, but yikes, he didn't crowd girls like me.

Oh my God. Oh my God. Oh my fucking God! What is happening?

Forrest lifted his hand, caressing my cheek. He brushed back a loose strand of my hair. I swallowed hard as I forced myself to look up.

"So, Sixx, you were telling me about your plans this weekend?"

I shook my head because I certainly had not been telling Forrest about my weekend plans. I had known him for most of my life, and he had been the cool jock. An unattainable jock that was just something to look at from afar. My first crush, but I had outgrown that, right? Right.

He had a chiseled jaw and robust features for a teenager, and he stood a head taller than most of the other guys in our class. His dirty blond hair that always managed to stay in the most recent style looked good on him. After growing up together, having classes, and being partnered once or twice, I wouldn't call him a friend. But I knew him. Heck, most of the kids in my class knew each other. We grew up together after all.

So, why the hell was he in my space, talking to me?

He leaned even closer, so close that I started to feel claustrophobic.

"Sixx." His voice dropped to a growly sound that made me want to run. After math yesterday, when our other pod mates joined our table, Ana and I hadn't been able to talk. Ana left fairly quickly with a wave, and I hadn't seen her since. This morning, when I walked to my locker, Forrest was already there, waiting for me. I really couldn't fathom why he was there. Or how he knew this was my locker since I told him mine was much further down. But there he was, leaning against *my* locker.

"What?" I blinked, lost in my thoughts.

He chuckled; his hand reached out to grab my waist, and I had to resist the temptation to slap his hand away. I rarely showed much interest in the guys here at my school.

I had known most of them for most of my life. I knew their dirty secrets. Dating here would have been fruitless and uninspiring. And right now, Forrest's interest was very uninvited.

Even if I was a bit of a romantic at heart, what teenage girl wasn't? But this situation didn't cause flutters of butterflies in my stomach, more like moths brushing against my skin. I shuddered. I hated—*hated*—moths. They terrified me after a horrid bonding camping trip that my parents took me on. We did all the classic routines, had a fire, roasted marshmallows. And when I went to bite into my perfectly built s'more, there was a fuzzy, hairy moth staring back at me. If that had been the end of it, I might have gotten over my fear. But no, it flew at me, which had me screaming, tumbling backward toward the fire.

Pain flared on my hip like the fire from my memory, but then I realized that the pain was fresh and very real. I refocused on the male towering over me. My heartbeat thundered in my ears—fear wrapped around me like a massive serpent. Yellow flared deep in his gaze, and fear from Saturday night came flooding back.

"Sixx, I need you to pay attention to me," Forrest growled.

How could I focus when my vision started to fade, blood draining from my face?

"What has that bitch, Anastasia, been telling you?" he snapped, moving a little closer, his hips pressing on mine. I hadn't even realized that I started to squirm, trying to get away, but my instincts screamed to get away from him as far as I could possibly go.

"Please get off of me, Forrest." I tried to look past his massive shoulders—too big for any teenager, by the way. But I couldn't see past them, and my chest tightened with my anxiety. I managed to put an inch between us. The weight of his body, the heat that flooded from him, started to suffocate me. As I struggled harder, a body squeezed between us. Though she was taller and lither than me, Ana had a presence about her that could not be ignored.

"Back off, Boris."

"I've told you a million times."

"Yeah, yeah, I know. Mind telling me why you are bothering my friend here?"

"That's between Sixx and me. Why do you feel the need to get involved, Anastasia?" he asked, voice dropping and his lips twisting in a sneer.

"Because my *friend* was uncomfortable, and a male was forcing himself on her," Ana said. It didn't escape me that she said male instead of man. Or even boy. But was that a habit of hers? I didn't have time to mull it over or even think about writing it down in my notebook.

In my notebook...oh...fuck.

The memory of his conversation with Nicole came crashing back. Not just that, but my missing sheets. There was no way. But he had dipped his head in close, nostrils flaring. Was he...scenting me? My head went light, and my knees practically gave out.

This was a whole new definition of Teenage Werewolf.

Holy hell.

"Well, maybe control your friend better," he snapped before stalking away. He glared over his shoulder at us once more. Ana waited until he was out of sight and his footsteps long went silent before she turned back to me.

"Ever skip school?" Ana asked as a mischievous smile overtook her features. I shook my head. This *female* would get me killed one day.

And that was how I found myself skipping school for the first time. We snuck into the bathroom that was the closest to one of the side entrances until the last warning bell went off. We ran out the side doors to Ana's car. It was a rusted old Jeep that looked like it had seen better days. When I climbed in, it groaned. I looked over at Ana, who just shrugged.

"Come on, we'll go for a drive. The school has ears," she said with a wink.

My eyes went wide, and I held my bag a little tighter, glad that I had it strapped over my shoulder when Forrest cornered me.

The further we got from the school, the more I realized I was in way over my head. This world was one I couldn't begin to comprehend. And after that encounter with Forrest, I seriously wondered how deeply the paras had a hold on this small town that seemed so sleepy before.

"What rabbit-hole did you just go down?" Ana asked as she gave me a sideways glance.

"Huh?"

"You were muttering. And not making a whole lot of sense."

"What exactly are you?" I asked. I cringed as she flinched. Because frankly, it came out harsher than I intended it to. It was just a lot to take in. It was one thing to read about this kind of world and pretend it was real. But to face it as reality?

I was terrified.

"I'm a girl, Sixx."

"You know what I mean," I snapped back, not appreciating her humor.

"Look, this isn't something I do. I don't go around telling people all my life-changing secrets all the time. I mean, do you?"

I didn't feel like I had life-changing secrets, but she had a point. I didn't go around telling people that I had only spoken to a couple of times that I had an irrational fear of moths. Or that my parents were mostly absent in my life and that I learned from a very young age about different types of love. And how to take care of myself.

"You're right, but…"

"You deserve to know what is going on in your backyard. Especially since I think that rogue that attacked you on Saturday caused quite a few ripples in the nearby pack. They are not happy, and they know it attacked someone. And they know someone stopped them."

My stomach twisted.

"Sixx, I can't be one hundred percent sure, but Forrest showing interest in you like he was…did he smell you?"

Shit.

"Shit."

"He did, didn't he?" Ana asked, her grip tightening on the steering wheel.

"Yeah."

"Okay, we will deal with that when the time comes. Well, I mean the time has come, but we will go to my aunt. She is aware that I had a tussle with a werewolf the other night. Hence why I was so exhausted this week. She has been running me through more training."

"Is she an ex-drill sergeant or something?" I joked.

"No, worse. She's a concerned guardian."

I managed to smile at that.

"We'll get you somewhat caught up on all things para, or at least give you a crash course, then go have a chat with my aunt. Unfortunately, I can tell you that there are a few paras in that school, and they have been watching me since I arrived."

"Why?"

"Our world has remained a secret, especially in this day and age with technology, because paras normally take care of things in-house. They decide the fate of those who find out their secret. And they keep things very tightly wrapped up. Punishments can be severe. They don't know me, and I came into their territory," Ana explained.

"Was there some type of protocol you were supposed to follow?" I asked because, as much as I knew it wasn't the time, my curiosity spiked.

"Not really? But honestly, I hadn't been expecting to run into any other paras in this little town. And if I am going to be honest with you, my aunt doesn't know about the paras in the school. She knew about the rogue because I can't very well hide the blood."

"Blood?" I paled, staring at the blond bombshell next to me.

"Yours, mine, a little bit, a lot bit of the rogue's."

I swallowed hard.

"Look, I am not saying I killed the monster, but the way that werewolf was going, he would have killed you."

I mulled that over for a minute. My mind caught onto one thing. If we were going to deal with her aunt, I didn't want to accidentally get us into more trouble than we already were in.

"Why didn't you tell your aunt about the paras at the school?"

"My aunt would have told me that we would need to leave and find somewhere else to be. I just wanted to finish my final year of high school in the place of my choosing. I didn't expect any of this to happen. I also didn't expect the paras to be so bold, but they're hotheaded idiots," Ana said, shaking her head.

"So, Forrest is one of them. Does that mean Nicole is, too?" I asked.

"How did you make that leap? Forrest makes sense, but how do you know about Nicole?" she asked, giving me a sideways glance.

"There are some things I meant to tell you," I said, guilt swamping me.

Chapter 7

We drove through town and got some sandwiches before driving up to the high point of Grand Haven. At night, it was where the "make-out" point used to be. A lot of parents still believed it happened there, so they would stalk it at night. Most kids didn't go there anymore. But it had a nice view, and much more importantly, it was private.

Ana and I sat on the hood of her Jeep, leaning against the windshield.

"You overheard Nicole and Forrest talking, but they didn't hear you? That's impressive," Ana said with a nod.

"I don't feel impressive. I feel over my head."

"Oh, don't get me wrong; you are," Ana said with a peal of laughter that could only be described as angelic. She bumped my shoulder as I shook my head. But it still didn't eliminate the fear that crept back in.

"What were they saying, do you remember?" Ana asked, getting us back on track.

"They were talking about scents, and someone was keeping things from them. Nicole said, 'It was her funky-ass scent,' I think?"

Ana cursed as she bit her thumbnail. She wiggled as if she wanted to get off the car and start pacing. I scooted a little away from her.

"That fucker needs to mind her own business."

"Why does Nicole have it out for you?"

Ana gave me a look.

"How do you know it's me?"

I gave her a look back that said—*puh-lease*. She laughed.

"She doesn't like me because I interrupt their perfect little world. I think Forrest doesn't or rather didn't mind me so much because I had been mostly sticking to my own business. But lately, they have been getting restless. I think it's been because of the wolf that attacked you the other night."

"Do you think the rogue followed you here?" I asked because before Ana, not that I blamed her, the paras in this town had gone undiscovered. I hadn't suspected anything strange about Forrest or even Nicole. They were just the popular kids that I had known most of my life. They lived their lives, and I lived mine. Or maybe I had been that oblivious.

"It's a possibility. But a lot of paras keep to their own business," Ana said as she unwrapped her sandwich. My stomach had been in knots since we left school—partly because I didn't skip – that just wasn't me – partly because of all of this new knowledge of a world that had been existing next to me forever.

"What I can't figure out is why Forrest cornered you this morning. I had been cautious to keep our conversations on more generic stuff."

She wasn't wrong about that. We discussed the movies we liked, and she told me about books she had been reading when she noticed the two in my bag. I had been close to finishing one and wanted to have another ready. Stuff that you asked people when you were trying to get a baser knowledge of an acquaintance.

"I think that was my fault again. I had been trying to do a bit of research myself. Also, I wanted to keep track of my thoughts and questions that I had, so I had been writing them down."

Ana dropped her head down, and her shoulders started to shake.

"Sixx, Sixx, Sixx," she muttered before throwing her head back and laughing. "You wrote down the questions? And did your research?"

"I like to be informed," I said, feeling a little prickly from her tone.

"No, I love it. Okay, well, bust that notebook out. And tell me what it has to do with Forrest suspecting you."

"I ran into Nicole on accident, and my stuff spilled out everywhere. I had a bit of information from things I found in the deep net about a monster-hunting group—as they call themselves. A picture of their seal and my first page of questions went missing. I had hoped that someone just picked it up and threw it away," I said, cringing a little. That sounded weak even to me.

"Sixx, I mean this with all the love that I have for you; that's asking *a lot* and is a tiny bit naïve."

"It was a lot of naïve, but I am also in the dark in this world. Knowledge is power, and you need to arm me," I said, sitting a little straighter. Ana nodded as she bit into her sandwich.

"No, those are all excellent points. So, I can give you a bit of information about the wolves, but I think it would be best if we discussed other things with my aunt."

"She won't be pissed that you are allowing a human into your house?" I asked, feeling a little strange using the term human like that. Like we both weren't, well...human.

"She is human. And I'm half-human. The other half is something we will need to ease you into," Ana said with a twinkle in her eye. I think she just liked the idea of holding off that information, letting me guess. My initial guess would be a witch because of the magic she had performed

Saturday night. It still boggled my mind that it had only been a week since this all went down.

"Okay, you were going to tell me about werewolves?"

"Forrest, Nicole, and a few others, sorry, no other names unless you figured it out yourself. The less you know of the specifics, the better off you will probably be. For now." Ana was placating me when I opened my mouth to argue that I needed to be aware of everyone in case I slipped. But when it came down to it, I couldn't slip. Not once, not ever.

"Werewolves have insane senses of smell. They don't follow the rules of the lore you probably think of. They don't just shift during full moons, but they are the strongest that night. Most creatures of the night are. There is power in it. But they have a lot of the characteristics of wolves. They live within pack units, and they have Alphas. The strongest lead, and the weaker ones are protected."

"Okay, so they don't sound like horrible beings." I nodded as I picked at my food.

Ana clenched her teeth together. The look she gave me said otherwise. My eyes widened.

"I thought you said they protected the weak."

"No, I said they protect their weaker ones. They don't have a whole lot of love for humans. As far as I am aware, they more than frown upon matings between werewolves and humans. Like they do not allow the wolf who mates with a human in their pack. Have you noticed if Forrest ever dates anyone outside of his circle?"

My brows bunched together as I considered that. I couldn't recall Forrest dating any of the girls in our school. He was a flirt for sure, but he didn't date.

"They don't like humans but live in a small town with a whole bunch of them as neighbors?" I questioned.

"Being a para is a very fine line. Humans outnumber paras by a lot. At least, here they do."

Here? As in our small town or as in...our world? But my brain wasn't ready to take on the possibility of a whole other plane of paranormal creatures.

"Most paras, from what I understand, respect the boundaries that allow us to live here, but some hate to live by the rules. There are good humans and bad ones. Some paras live their lives the best they can, but there are those who like to toe the line. Or just bolt right past it."

I nodded as I listened. A small part of me felt a pang of sadness at the idea of my romanticized vision of her world. There would be no fated mates happening here, or beautiful, long-lasting love that would span over paras to humans.

"Sorry it's not a more beautiful view."

"It's reality, not fiction," I said. The disappointment of reality was something I had become very familiar with after my grandmother passed away when I had been five. She had been my father's mother. My father tried his best, but as the holidays approached, he had been overwhelmed. A plump little child that had dreams of Santa bringing her grandmother back had been too much for him. He snapped at me one day and revealed that Santa wasn't real and my grandmother could never return.

He apologized later and tried to repair the damage, but that was irreparable. I allowed those memories to fade away as Ana took a massive bite of her sandwich. I wanted to ask how she could eat right now, but her world didn't just explode.

"You called that wolf a rogue a couple of times. What does that mean?"

"The definition of a rogue is a being that is off on their own. You should know that." Ana said.

"You know what I meant."

"Yeah, yeah. A rogue werewolf is one that has separated from the pack. Some do it because they want to join a new pack and are just in between. Others are born lone wolves, but those are extremely rare. Werewolves need a pack to survive. And they take care of their own. But if a rogue has lost their senses because they have been out of pack life too long and if they expose themselves...those involved tend to disappear. Including the wolf. But werewolves are fiercely protective of their land as well.

"This is their land. And they will do anything to keep their secrets, well, a secret," Ana said with a shrug as if it was nothing. But it was everything. The thought I had earlier rang even truer now than it had been then.

"So my knowing is a massive problem?"

"Probably. But we will talk to my aunt. If there is anyone to help us out of this situation, it will be her."

Ana and I climbed off the hood of her car, and I threw away the remaining pieces of my food. Ana ate all of hers. We climbed into the car, and I saw the worry crossing her features.

"Will your aunt hurt me?" I asked. If I had to live the rest of my life on eggshells, not speaking about what I knew, I would do it. But I wanted to be able to live my life.

"No. I promise, Sixx. She wouldn't."

The pang of fear I felt faded as I snapped my seatbelt in place.

"She might put a spell on you, though."

"What?" I chirped, grabbing onto the door handle, ready to dive out of the car to relative safety.

"I'm kidding. Sorry, Sixx. You are going to find out that I like to joke around with my friends. I mean, you are probably my first official one, but still, I'm enjoying it."

I smiled back. Was I her only friend? There was no way. She had a large personality that would win anyone over. But I had a feeling, from the little she had exposed to me about her world, that she was being honest. It sounded like secrecy was her life.

"Well, I hope, at the very least, she doesn't get upset with you."

"Oh, she is already pissed at me. I'm not worried about it. But since she'll be the only other *full* human in the room, it would probably be best for her to explain everything that you need to know about keeping unnoticed."

Thoughts ran through my head, and there were things I needed to ask, needed to get out of the way, but my head kept spinning back to the same thought—the other human.

Chapter 8

"Anastasia Dotty Cooper. What the fuck have you done?"

"Um, ma'am."

Steely gray eyes shifted to me.

"I know you did not just *ma'am* me! Don't think because I don't know you, you aren't in serious trouble yourself," the slightly younger, more muted version of Ana said. She had the same blond hair, but it was limper than Ana's as the stress of her day pressed it down close to her skull. Her cheeks were slightly sunken and stretched over her bones. I think we aged her twenty years in a matter of minutes.

I snapped my mouth shut, sitting a little straighter. Ana looked over me with a hint of disbelief and amusement. I glared at her then shifted my gaze back to her aunt, who started to pace in front of us.

Ana had brought us back to the small rental. It was a quaint, little, two-bedroom cottage. We walked into the mismatched living room that had a lavender-colored, two-seater couch. A bright yellow comfy chair rounded out the area around a refurbished fireplace with a TV mounted over the mantel.

The light coloring on the walls and the accents made the place seem utterly cheerful compared to the occupants' very stormy features. Ana's aunt raked her hand through her hair for what seemed like the hundredth time.

"Okay, tell me again what *really* happened on Saturday," Lola said as she stopped in front of us. She was rail-thin, her jeans tight around her legs but a little loose at the waist. Life on the run with her para niece didn't seem to agree with her much. A pang of sadness hit me thinking about the life she had to sacrifice for this chaotic one. That was true love.

"I was out for a run when I heard screaming and rustling. When I found the source, I discovered a rogue werewolf attacking Sixx. I couldn't just let it kill her! So I intervened." Ana shrugged as if it was the most natural thing in the world to save my life. I didn't think Lola wanted to see me dead, but at the same time, her niece put a lot on the line by helping me. Then, I screwed her over by accidentally outing both of us.

"Was Sixx the only witness?" Lola asked, her steely gaze back on her niece.

"No," Ana whispered, looking away from both of us.

"The rogue is still alive?" Lola asked.

My head spun at that. Were they so casually talking about Ana killing another being? Even if that being had attacked me and seemed a little crazed, it wasn't…No. My chest tightened, and it became hard to breathe.

Unfortunately, when I hit a certain level of anxiety, I start to cry. It was frustrating but unavoidable. If I could figure out a way to make it stop, I would. As I struggled not to burst into tears around Ana and her aunt, whom I met two minutes ago, they continued to talk.

"I wounded the rogue, but I didn't have any weapons with me. Plus, I heard a werewolf on our trail. I would have stuck around and hid to make sure, but I wanted to get back to check on Sixx."

"And you have been sitting on this since last weekend? What would you have done if she told people what happened?"

Ana looked guilty, nervous even.

"Oh, fuck, what did you do?" Aunt Lola said, her gaze dragging back to me. I made a choked noise in the back of my throat. It was not only the weight of her stare but the fact she brazenly swore at two teenagers. Not that we hadn't heard worse at school. But it was jarring to hear it from an adult.

"I might have written out just a few questions to ask Ana. And done a little bit of research," I whispered, refusing to look her aunt in the eye. Out of the corner of my eye, I saw Lola pinch the bridge of her nose.

"Okay, what?"

"That was probably my fault, too, Aunt Lola."

"Why didn't you tell me about what was happening before? We could have brought Sixx in earlier," Lola said as she started to pace in front of us again. I squirmed in my seat, feeling uncomfortable.

"Is there any possibility that we could all just forget that I know anything and I just go home?" I muttered, feeling overwhelmed. My heart pounded in my chest.

"Sorry, Sixx. It would be best if you stayed here for the night. We need to figure out a game plan now that you know. Please, tell me that you have all the information you wrote down with you?"

Ana nudged me as if she wanted me to keep my mouth sealed shut. But when Lola's sharp gaze met mine, I sat up a little straighter and cleared my throat.

"No," I croaked.

"No, you don't have everything with you? Or no...?"

"No?"

"That's not an answer. Anastasia."

"She might have lost a page or two, but it had nothing that would be dangerous for anyone who didn't know what they were looking for," Ana said with a shrug of her shoulder. She looked practically bored as she leaned back in her seat. Lola narrowed her eyes.

"And those werewolves from the pack haven't caused you any issues?" she asked.

"No, I told you that I have them under control. They think that Sixx has been tutoring me. They want to keep their secret as much as I want to keep mine. We have an understanding."

My brows pinched together. She didn't even tell her aunt that the werewolves at school had been bothering her. Threatening her? But maybe it was the same as any high school drama, the new girl drawing too much attention?

Lola sighed before shaking her head.

"You're both horrible liars. Look, the safest option is for Sixx to stay with us tonight, and I will have to give you a crash course in all things para. But it's been a long day, week, I'm sure. You two go get ready for bed, and I will sort out what I need to go through with you, Sixx."

"Come on, Sixx." Ana grabbed my elbow and urged me to stand. Her aunt disappeared into the kitchen while Ana led me upstairs. There were two bedrooms on that level; one was sparse, and we walked right past it.

The other bedroom that Ana led me into had a light gray comforter and clothes spread out through the room. There was a laundry basket filled with clothes that belonged to Ana. She immediately released me and started to pick at the different discarded clothes.

"I don't think anything of yours will fit me," I muttered because that seemed like the biggest issue right now. Hell, even her aunt was petite. None of the clothes in this house would fit me. And I didn't have my homework. My parents had no idea where I would be. Not that I thought that was the biggest concern, but at the same time...

"Forrest and Nicole know me. They have known me for most of my life. They can figure out where I live. What about my parents?" I screeched, jerking toward the door. Ana moved faster than lightning and blocked the exit.

"You need to calm down. Trust me when I say they are not going to involve any more people than they have to. The werewolves aren't stupid," Ana said as she held my shoulders. Her gaze locked on mine, a bright unnatural blue glowing from them. My hammering heart slowed. My focus became singular.

"What are you?" I asked. There was a dreamy edge to my voice that I recognized wasn't natural. Ana cringed and took a step back, breaking our eye contact. A shiver went down my spine. Blinking, I tried to get a sense of my space again—Ana's small room with her full-size bed that took up half the room. The floor was still covered with her clothes and the laundry basket. The walls were a pale lavender color that didn't seem to fit the girl in front of me. But she was an anomaly for sure.

Ana moved through the room, picking up an oversized shirt, and brought it to her nose. Something inside of me cracked. I couldn't stop the snort that escaped me or the irresistible bubbling of laughter from my stomach outward.

I leaned over, clutching my stomach as I tried to control my laughter, but every time I peeked up to see Ana, with her platinum blond hair and supermodel good looks, I just started to laugh again.

"This is not how I ever imagined my life going," I said, slapping my knee after another bout of laughter.

Ana just raised her brows at me as she lowered the shirt from her nose.

"I will admit this is not my most glamorous moment. But I also have just been trying to get through senior year."

And that started another round of laughter from me. This time, Ana joined in as she glanced down at the shirt.

"I will admit, I didn't think this was how my weekend would go."

I shook my head as I collapsed on the bed. Ana joined me, lying next to me.

"I'm sorry that you've been roped into this," Ana said. Our laughter seemed to leave an echo around the room as we both caught our breaths.

"So, you didn't imagine a kickass, para type combing through her room trying to find something clean for you to wear?"

"Nope. But I also thought my life would have kept this sort of mess inside of books. You know, where it belongs."

Ana got a look on her face before she smiled brightly at me.

"What's that they always say, never meet your heroes? I guess I know why we aren't very prepared for visitors."

I mustered another laugh for her.

"Come on, Aunt Lola will have her presentation ready by now, I'm sure. And maybe we can find something for you to wear, sorry." Ana cringed as she looked around her room. I think she genuinely thought something of hers might fit me, but her clothes were dirty. I shrugged because I would do with what I had. We had bigger fish to fry.

Ana and I returned downstairs to hear her aunt pacing in the kitchen. We rounded the corner, and I took a seat at the small, mismatched dinner table that they had tucked in the kitchen. It looked like it was due for an upgrade, but my guess was this was just a temporary spot for Lola and Anastasia.

"First thing you need to know about the para world..."

"Is no one talks about the para world?" I quipped, unable to help myself. The way I grew up, I found myself looking for different outlets. Movies that had accrued a cult following had always been an interest for me. It meant having a connection with someone who didn't know me but knew me because of our shared interests.

"I know you are trying to make a joke, but you are not wrong," Ana said, laughing behind her hand. Her aunt looked less thrilled by my joke. I just offered a sheepish smile and zipped my lips shut. Lola shook her head and started up again.

"Yes, we don't discuss it outside this house. Paras are very secretive for a good reason. They keep their identities close to their hearts. I can't express the danger that you are in now that you know. And if any of those werewolves that might have caught your scent find out who you are..."

The threat lingered in the air, but Lola didn't need to flat out say it.

I was dead.

Chapter 9

"There are a lot of rules to go over, but you are both here for the night. And I think if I drop any more truths, Sixx is going to keel over," Lola said, squinting at me. The blood had rushed from my cheeks as my head kept spinning over *death.*

I still had a whole life ahead of me. Death was a concept that belonged to long ago lost grandparents. I had my share of death, I understood it, but it wasn't something I would seriously consider. Yet, I recalled each moment running from the crazed wolf, and my heart slammed inside of my chest.

Death by claws.

Death by jaws.

Death by classmates who barely even knew I existed. The only reason they showed any interest in me lately had been because of Ana. Not that I blamed her for the decisions of others, but nausea pooled in my mouth.

"I might be sick."

"Understandable," Lola said as matter-of-factly as she could, empathizing with a nod. Ana rolled her eyes where she sat next to me.

"You aren't helping, Aunt Lola."

"I'm not trying to. The sooner you realize the danger you put her in, the better. And the sooner she realizes the best thing to do is to keep her head down and get the hell out of dodge, the better. I'm sorry, Sixx, but your life is never going to be the same. I'm not going to sugarcoat it."

"Maybe you should," Ana mumbled.

"Like I got it sugar-coated to me?" Lola snapped. As she yelled, I didn't realize before that she favored one leg over the other. Not to mention her hair covered one side of her neck, but when she leaned forward, I saw the scar that marred her skin. Ana looked down, ashamed, but still had a sense of defensiveness about her.

And as I watched them, I couldn't help but put myself in Ana's shoes. She had told me before that her life had been a pretty lonely existence. Lola was the only person in her life who knew her secret; hell, I didn't even really know her secret. Ana wanted someone that she could talk to, someone who understood. A friend. "That..."

"I'm sorry, I didn't mean to snap at you, Ana. This was never on you. That was wrong of me," Lola said, pulling her niece in for a hug. I looked away, trying to give them a bit of privacy for what seemed like an old wound.

"It's been a long night. I will go pick up a pizza, and we will talk more when I get back. I don't think it needs to be said, but just in case, don't fucking leave," Lola added.

Ana smiled at her aunt. "Not even…"

"Not even. Look, keep her safe. That's all I am asking. And I'm probably paranoid, but I will feel better if I can be here with you two. Pull out whatever weapon you feel most comfortable with. Sixx, I am going to go out on a limb and say you have no formal training?"

"Uh…"

I blinked at her a couple of times before she shook her head.

"Yeah, nope. Didn't think so. Okay, protect her," Lola said. I opened my mouth to object but quickly shut it. What would I be able to do? Blow them away with my useless knowledge of books I've read and my references to obscure movies?

Lola left with another stern warning for us to remain in the house. I didn't know where she thought we would go. Bowling? The thought made me snort under my breath, which resulted in Ana giving me side-eye. I waved her away. I'd tell her later after her aunt was out of earshot. I didn't think she would see the humor in my thoughts.

After Lola left, we both breathed a tiny bit easier. For me, Lola scared me because she was the authority figure here. She represented the truth and the weight of the situation we were in. Not that it left my mind, but it was easier to think that this wasn't as dire when it was just Ana and me. Who would willingly hurt two seemingly innocent teenagers?

The only crime I truly committed was nothing. They were laws made by creatures that shouldn't exist.

"What made you laugh?" Ana asked as we milled toward the living room.

"Your aunt seemed worried that we would leave, and I wondered where we would go, and the only thought that came to mind was bowling."

Ana gave me an odd look before she shook her head.

"You're a strange cookie, but I dig it."

"Thank you?" I questioned, but she just waved me over to sit with her.

"I'm sorry about my aunt. She can be a little intense."

"A little?" I choked out.

"Okay, a lot, but she has her reasons."

"Do you know who your parents are?" I asked, stepping into dangerous territory. Ana got quiet, and she looked over at a framed picture of her and her aunt. She'd told me before that her aunt was her mother's true blood sister. But what happened to her? What of her father?

"The only family I know or care about is that woman. My aunt has been my everything."

And I recognized a closed door when I heard one. My parents used that tone with me enough that I knew when to back off. Instead, I focused on the picture she was looking at. Ana didn't seem that much younger, but her aunt seemed significantly different. She seemed more lively, glowing, her hair thick, and she just looked stunning.

I wondered what had brought them here to our little town from their previous stop.

"Want to watch this? It's my aunt and my go-to when we just need something to pass the time," Ana asked, queuing up one of my favorite sitcoms. I smiled brightly and got a little cozier on the couch.

"Yes, please."

I curled up on the couch with my feet tucked under my butt while Ana spread out. Time flew; we both ended up speaking lines together, which was immediately followed by our laughter. The stress of the day started to unwind from my shoulders, and I could pretend that I was having a relaxing evening with a new friend.

Ana sat up in between episodes, her head tilting to the side. She grabbed the remote without really looking at the TV, her attention elsewhere. I sat up and tried to listen to what she was hearing. The best I could do was the noise from the show even as she turned it down.

"Shit. Run upstairs and hide," Ana said, her voice sharp with command. I didn't think I just reacted. But because I was sitting, I stumbled off the couch, my foot getting caught in the blanket. My head went rushing toward the side of the coffee table, but Ana managed to grab me and throw me back onto the couch.

The front door burst open as she did, and I screamed.

There was something to be said about how you thought you would react in a terrifying situation versus how you did. It turned out I had no chill when it came to those sorts of situations. My brain went completely blank. All I could think was someone was breaking in.

Someone broke in.

Ana handled it like a pro, moving with the grace of a dancer and the ferocity of a warrior. She grabbed something close to her that looked like a decorative stick, which I realized now was strategically placed there. She brandished her staff-like weapon, making herself the apparent threat in the room.

Two beast-like things stepped into the room. Coarse, stringy hair covered their bodies. One dropped from two legs back down to four, while the other remained on all four. The second one dropped its head between its shoulders. Nostrils flared as it swept the room.

Werewolves.

My mouth went dry, and I finally stopped screaming. Instead, pathetic little whimpers were ripped from my throat as I scrambled backward as its yellow eyes latched onto me.

A thick stick dropped between us. I blinked, looking at Ana, who kept her focus on the two beasts, but her message was clear.

I needed to get my ass moving now.

Crawling over the couch, I made it to the furthest side of it before my feet hit the hardwood. I peeked over my shoulder before taking off. Ana still held off both of the beasts, but something told me that they were just toying with us. Especially when the one that had been watching me flashed its teeth at me when I took one more look over my shoulder.

My heart pounded so hard in my chest that I thought it would burst through. My lungs squeezed as it became difficult to breathe beyond my panic. Nails scraped against the hardwood behind me. Everything in me screamed not to look back, but pure fear motivated me.

Craning my neck, I peeked over my shoulder and regretted it. The darker of the two wolves, the one that had been watching me, leaped forward. I stumbled up the stairs as he knocked against the wall, moving too fast.

I screamed again, finding my voice once more. But in my mad dash, my shin hit the stairs and knocked me off course. I stumbled backward into biting range. The wolf snapped its jaws, and I noticed it was foaming at the mouth.

"Oh my God, oh my God, oh my God," I muttered as I kicked out at the wolf's jaw. I probably only managed to piss the thing off, but I'd rather do that than allow it to grab onto me.

I couldn't hear what was happening on the other side of the house with Ana and her opponent. Then, I wondered how long it would take for Lola to return. Would they hurt her, too? Would they recognize that she was Ana's guardian and leave her be?

My distraction cost me because the wolf was not distracted by my wayward thoughts. Instead, it lunged, grabbing a mouthful of my jeans and pulling me down the stairs. My head knocked against the risers, and I cried out in pain.

It didn't soften the wolf to my cause. Instead, it seemed to rile the beast even more. He released me as soon as my butt hit the tile of the kitchen floor. He growled when I started to crawl back up the stairs. I stopped my movements. My entire body ached. I didn't know what it wanted.

To play with its meal? Meaning me?

Was it just trying to draw this out?

I leaned forward to try to gauge where Ana was. Could I get a hit in that would afford me enough time for her to help me?

The wolf lunged forward, forcing my attention back to it. I jerked backward as its hot, ragged breath brushed against my cheek. I couldn't stop the whimper or the tears that streaked down my cheeks. My heart about gave out when it chuffed a wolfy-like laugh and decided to do it once more.

This time, my head hit the stairs hard enough that my vision went black.

Chapter 10

"You weren't supposed to kill her."

"I didn't, you idiot. She doesn't smell like death."

Thinking better of myself, I groaned. My mouth felt like it was filled with cotton. A searing pain jolted down the front of my head, and I curled up on myself.

"See, she is moving. She's still alive," one of the male voices boasted.

"You should be so proud. Taking two teenage girls to their deaths because you are too weak to do it yourselves," Ana spat. It was wrong to feel a bit of relief at hearing her voice, but I did. I squinted one eye open to take in our surroundings. A jarring bump made me groan a little louder. Cringing, everything inside of me wanted this to end. The nausea, the pain, and the fear coiled inside of me, tightening to the point it felt physical.

My hands shook as I tried to calm myself down. But the more I thought about it, the more terrified I became. I was only seventeen, working on my way to eighteen. My biggest concern should be whether I would go to prom with my friends or skip the whole thing. I was spiraling.

"Shut up, Halfling. You brought this upon yourselves," one of the males snapped.

A sob choked in my throat. Halfling? Was I learning more things than I should because they thought I was still passed out? If I could get away with maybe like a forgetting spell or something since I knew so little, I would take the deal.

"Excuse me for existing," Ana growled, hatred filling her tone. It had been selfish for me to think only of myself. What would happen to her? It didn't sound like these two had a whole lot of love for whatever Ana was.

The only thing that I took comfort in, and maybe a bit of disappointment, was that neither sounded like Forrest. Perhaps if he was here, we could reason with him. My heart tripped in my chest when the silence thickened.

"We know you are awake, human," one of the males snarled.

"I wasn't trying to hide it," I muttered, still unable to uncurl myself from my position. Ana scooted closer, but she didn't reach out. I cracked my eyes open a little more, only to see that she was handcuffed to the railing on the inside of the van. This had been specially made for their use, which made my stomach tighten even more.

"Lock her up on the other side. We don't know what they are capable of together. And the Alpha wants them brought to him as quickly as possible."

That we weren't there already surprised me. Surely, I had been knocked out for a while, right? But as one of the werewolves stepped into the back, I retreated, getting closer to Ana. He watched me with a snarl on his lips. Well, if he had been in my position, I think he'd have reacted the same way. This wasn't something ordinary people dealt with.

I was kidnapped, for fuck's sake.

"I'll find a way out of this, Sixx. I promise."

I peeked up at Ana, who spoke with such strength that I hated myself for the fear that ruled over me. She was the same age, and even if she belonged to this world, somehow, I doubted her protective aunt had allowed her to be kidnapped before this. She probably had as much experience with kidnapping as I did.

The werewolf seemed angrier as he reached for me, and I cringed away from him. He gripped my elbow too tightly and roughly pulled me away from Ana. They'd seated me across from her, but for some reason, it felt safer if we sat side by side.

He was not kind as he zip-tied my wrist to an adjacent bar along the van's inside. The plastic bit into my fragile skin. I twisted in my seat, unable to sit still. The wolf watched me before he ducked his head and returned to the passenger seat.

Swallowing hard, I looked over at Ana, trying to push down the rising panic in my chest. It squeezed like a vice, making it harder and harder to breathe.

"Hey, Sixx, why did the bike fall over?"

I stopped my struggling and just blinked at Ana, convinced that she'd lost her mind.

"What?" I squeaked.

"Because…it was two tired."

Crickets would have been appropriate. Even the low hum of the radio couldn't break the silence between us better. I lifted one side of my mouth, posed to ask if she lost her mind.

"Okay, that one was a little lame. Let me try again." Ana brought her hand in front of her face, recomposing herself before sitting a little straighter.

"Why did the mushroom go to the party?"

Ana waited a second before she started to laugh at her unanswered joke. I think? When she managed to stop laughing for a second, she looked at me with a twinkle in her eye.

"Cause, Sixx, get this. He was a…fungi."

"Um…"

"Oh, come on, I think stooge number two up there cracked a smile at that one," Ana said, smiling even if her laugh was a bit manic. Or maybe I was projecting because I couldn't find any humor in this situation. I couldn't find a trace of the calm that she exuded.

"No, I don't think he did," I muttered, feeling sick to my stomach.

For a split second, I expected one of the two in the front to weigh in, but they were both quiet. Could they hear everything we were saying? I simply didn't have enough knowledge to know how to handle this situation. Fiction was great and all, and all those heroines acted just like Ana, unafraid. They quipped and joked and knew they had an out. I feared my out wouldn't be as pleasant.

The drive was quiet after that. I think Ana felt a little defeated at my deflated sense of humor.

Thanks to the fact that I was either still stressed or still concussed, but darkness took me under.

****

The slow rocking of the van woke me. And unlike all those times I read in books, I didn't get that small reprieve when I forgot everything that had happened in the last couple of hours and got to live in a moment of peace. No, I woke, knowing the fate that awaited both Ana and me. Which made it infinitely harder to want to open my eyes.

After all, I couldn't face what was next blind. I didn't think well on the fly. It wasn't a strength of mine. I was one of those people who, when faced with a test, felt my entire mind went blank. What had I even learned through the whole year? Who knew?

The ride had been mostly uneventful besides being tied to the inside of the van. And there were Ana's attempts at joking, which might have been a bit of torture itself. But I smiled at the effort she put into trying to calm me. My neck ached from sleeping at such a strange angle, and when I lifted my head to look over at her, I saw the flash of fear she must have been hiding.

I wanted to believe she was this badass heroine who feared nothing, that this would be a walk in the park for her, but her knees were tucked close to her chest. She rested her cheek on her knee with unshed tears in her eyes.

"Hey, what do you call a hornless unicorn?"

Ana looked over at me, raising a brow.

"A horse."

"That was by far the worst joke ever," she said with a smile and a light reentering her eyes that had been dimmed a moment before. My heart squeezed. We were in this together, and I had to remember that. I couldn't just let her take the wheel because she was more capable. Because she was, but I needed to remain strong, too—even the strongest people buckled under the weight of the world.

The van slowed even more, and I couldn't stop the fear that iced my veins. I leaned forward to try to peek out the windshield, but darkness greeted me. Ana followed suit and grabbed my free hand.

"Together," she whispered. I nodded.

I had been close to a couple of my friends that I had known for most of my life. I could recite their favorite colors, candy, what kind of movies they preferred. But the connection I felt with Ana right then was different. We had promised to keep each other safe. Whatever happened next, our lives were entwined together.

The guys from the front of the van climbed out. I saw one of them lift his nose into the air as if he was scenting it.

"They probably brought us to the forest. Paras are strange about their laws. I haven't had to deal with it much. My aunt knows a bit more than I do. I think she has a contact that helped her through some sticky situations. I am not great with my powers. But I promise, Sixx, we will get out of this together."

I could sense the guilt in her words. She felt partially responsible for the situation we were in. But in the end, we had no one to blame but the rogue werewolf who attacked me. And honestly, the blame was on me. If I hadn't been foolish enough to write down my questions, let my curiosity get the better of me, we wouldn't be in this situation.

"Werewolves have better senses even in their human form, so be very careful what information you give. Even when you think we are alone, I don't think we will be.

You're in too deep to let you just go on as you are. But the amount of information you have will determine the severity of what will happen," Ana explained as quickly as she could. She spoke in barely one breath to get it all out before the doors in the back of the van opened.

The night air, crisp and fresh, rushed in. Instead of giving me a sense of relief, dread followed. Spikes poked in the inside of my stomach, and I wanted to hunch over and hold it. The pain wouldn't retreat. The werewolf came into the van and sliced Ana's zip-tie without a knife, instead using wicked sharp claws that transformed his hand. I tried not to let my eyes bug out of their sockets as I observed his partial shift.

He moved quickly, ushering her out of the back of the van where the driver waited. He had been the one who remained a mystery to me. The one with the partial shift turned his attention back to me. He had been the one to tie me here and, if I had to guess, the one who knocked me out in the house. However, that had been my doing as well.

He looked young, but what did I know about para aging? Was it like the books where werewolves aged slower than humans? Did they age out about the same? Did it matter in this situation? Not really, but part of me wanted to humanize him, to make him see me as human.

"Please, you and your friend can just let us go. We won't talk about what happened. My name is..."

"Shut up," he growled, not being careful as he slashed my zip-tie. There was more brutality to his treatment of me than Ana. He grabbed my elbow again, which had been bruised by him already, and yanked me out of the van. Ana gave me a shaky smile.

How much had she heard of me trying to plead with him?

"Let's get going. The Alpha will be here soon," the driver said, holding onto Ana. He had some of the same colorings as the guy holding me. Both seemed way too young to be holding hostages. My guard had a weak chin, which he tried to cover with barely-there stubble. His eyes were hard and empty.

The driver holding Ana could have been considered attractive if not a little too old for both of us. He looked like he was in his mid-twenties but had a stubborn line to his jaw. This was a job for him. He wanted this over and done with.

Chapter 11

The walk through the dark forest was not something I ever wanted to relive. The other three moved with a lot more ease and grace than I could manage even on a well-lit day and a clear path. The trees blocked out the moonlight, which made me squint even harder. It didn't help that, when the werewolf had pushed me out of the back of the van, my glasses had gone flying. Even with them, I wouldn't have been able to see.

The limbs on the ground threatened to trip me every shuffle forward. Ana tried to slow her pace so she walked with me. She tried to help direct me, but apparently, the werewolves thought we were up to something and separated us again.

"Oof." I tripped and stubbed my toe against a thick root. I fell forward, throwing my hands out to catch myself. The werewolf who had been holding onto my elbow allowed me to fall. As I slammed to the ground, the wind was practically knocked out of my lungs. The group stopped as I gasped.

Light sparked and sizzled. My gaze went to Ana, who watched with anger. Electricity sparked in her eyes. Rage lined her every moment, and her shoulders tensed as her fist tightened dangerously. Power swirled around her, thickening the air.

The werewolf holding her snarled at her but jerked his hands away when power crackled over her arms. The guard watching over me turned his attention to her. Ana's face melted to a mask of indifference. A glazed look crossed over her eyes. Her lips pressed tightly together as more power swelled around her.

My mind screamed to run, somewhere, anywhere. The safest place should be by her side, but my instincts said nope. I scrambled backward as the wind whipped around us, the trees creaking at the sudden gusting vortex.

My guard noticed that I started to back away and lunged forward to grab me. Ana's unfocused gaze skipped over to us as I tried to crab crawl backward from the werewolf. His canines grew as he peeled back his lips.

The one watching Ana finally reacted, coming out of his stupor. He rushed her, thinking she was distracted. I swallowed hard, opening my mouth to call out a warning to her, but it cost me precious seconds to put space between my assailant and me.

The werewolf gripped my naked ankle with elongated claws that bit deep into my skin. I yelped as red-hot pain spiked through my leg. He growled as he yanked me back. My fingers dug into the ground; dirt raked under my nails. They ripped and tore as I clawed, trying to find purchase.

The wind spiked, and instead of icy pinpricks, it became suffocating. Heat twisted in the wind, making it harder to focus. I glanced over at Ana. Vivid blue crackling pulsed over her entire body. The wolf who tried to contain her was knocked back by the force of the wind around her.

"Get the bitch," one snapped at the other. I could barely focus. I was screaming as the pain continued to rip through my leg. His claws punctured my jeans like butter and split through to the skin and muscle. His nails left gouges in my skin. My heart slammed in my throat when he yanked me closer.

I screamed when his claws punctured around my knee.

Ana's attention turned back to us, and she took a step forward. I kicked my leg out, trying to dislodge the werewolf crawling up it. My heart slammed in my throat. I managed to get him off when a thick branch flew overhead. He ducked to avoid it while Ana shot an arm forward. An electric blue bolt whipped from her extended hand. But her eyes widened as the bolt released and went out of her control.

The bolt shot straight toward me. I screamed as I tried to roll out of the way, but it shot through me. I had never been tased before, never even thought about how it would feel. This made sure I *never* wanted to be on the sparky end of a taser ever.

My entire body jerked, muscles contracting painfully. I tried to scream, but the tendons in my neck were so strained that I couldn't even muster a whimper.

"Shit!" Ana's voice broke through as the wind died down. Hands clamped down on my arms and lifted me upward. I couldn't resist; my muscles were still locked down, and exhaustion swamped my mind.

Ana collapsed on her knees, panting heavily as she looked over at me. Her werewolf guard had his hand gripped around the back of her neck, his black claws digging into her skin.

"If you continue to use your magic, she'll pay the price," he growled, nodding his head in my direction. As if to drive that point home, the man behind me pushed his knee into the back of mine. I fell, my muscles like noodles, but his claws dug deep into my flesh. I swallowed back the shout of pain.

Ana noticed and jerked forward.

"Leave her be, and I won't use my magic," Ana surrendered.

"Stephen, take her to the cave. I don't trust them together any longer," the werewolf holding Ana snarled, his hand tightening on her neck.

"Come on, human," Stephen said, dragging me along.

The rest of the walk was mostly uneventful. I kept tripping, but Stephen made sure to keep an iron grip on me. There was a small inlet where a den had been tucked around thick greenery. The hillside looked like something out of a show. I didn't think perfect carved dens like this existed in real life. But the closer we got, the more I wondered if they used magic to create the outlet.

Those thoughts disappeared when he forced me into the pitch-black cavern. The temperature dropped significantly as goosebumps erupted over my skin. A full-body shiver wracked through me. Stephen moved without any issues, but the further we went in, the more cracks and lifts had me stumbling worse than on the forest floor.

He stopped, releasing me. I wanted to bolt, but in the absolute darkness, with my luck, I would run right into a wall. Whipping his hand out, he gripped my wrist as cold metal knocked against my bone painfully. A loud click echoed around the cavern.

My stomach plummeted as he dropped my wrist, which was heavily weighed down. I lifted my wrist closer to my face, but I couldn't see anything. The cold metal against my skin was enough of an indicator, though. The best I got was the reflective glow of Stephen's eyes as he moved closer to me.

"Don't worry, you won't be alone for long," he whispered before his footsteps retreated away from me. Fear swept through me. It felt more like a warning than anything else. He didn't care for my comfort or Ana's. That made me wonder if they would take her somewhere else.

If he left the cavern entirely, I had no idea. However, the adrenaline that had kept me alert up to that point faded out as my heart had a moment to settle. Not that these conditions were at all ideal, but it gave me a moment to breathe. With that, the pain in my leg flared, and the encompassing darkness swallowed me whole. And reality settled around me.

This could very well be how I died.

I reached out, my hands scraping against the hard, rocky surface as I used that leverage to fall to the ground. Curling up on the cold stone, I touched my leg. It came back wet. I whimpered, unsure what to do. Keeping it from the dirty surface had been my best bet.

My jeans were torn to pieces from the knee down, but the best I could do was by touch. I didn't know how dirty my hands were after everything, and probing my wounds with dirt-covered hands didn't seem like a good idea.

The cavern silence was deafening. Only minutes had passed since Stephen left, but my mind screamed it had been longer. *Hours.* What if they did keep Ana and me separated?

Panic squeezed at my lungs as it became harder to breathe.

Chapter 12

Anastasia

Fuck. Fuck. Fuuuck.

This was all my fault. And worse, I unintentionally gave them more information about what I was than I had intended to. I hadn't wanted them to know about my magic, but I lost my temper when they abused Sixx. It didn't take a lot for me to lose my temper when someone weaker than I was being attacked. Even worse, I liked Sixx. She was unique. I thought about how she tried to come to my rescue a couple of times already. It had been a long time since I allowed myself to become friends with someone.

Aunt Lola had encouraged me to make friends when I was younger. And for a good while, I did. But then we would have to leave. Either another para took notice, or my aunt needed a change of scenery. At least that was what she said, but I realized that we moved for my protection. And hers.

The danger I was in was significantly different from the danger she was in, which terrified me. I never wanted anything bad to happen to her, not for taking me in. For raising me, for being my only family. And this time, I fucked things up.

But now, I not only put my aunt in danger but Sixx, too. She didn't deserve what these werewolves had planned for her. Most of the packs we had run into in the past usually kept to themselves, but they guarded their secret with a vicious bite.

When we arrived in this town, I recognized the younger werewolves in the school. I just wanted to finish out the school year without moving in the middle of the year again. And even as much as Aunt Lola tried to hide it, something was wrong with her. Her health was declining, and she needed to find a place to rest.

I could handle the younger werewolves as long as they did their own thing and I did mine. The only reason Forrest started to get weird was because Nicole saw me use a bit of magic in school. I think she didn't like the idea of another para in the school. Werewolves dated outside of their packs, but rarely did they find their mates outside of other packs. I think little missy saw me as a bit of competition, which was stupid. I didn't want a werewolf boyfriend ever. No, far too possessive and protective. I'd never see the light of day again.

"The human is locked up," the werewolf named Stephen said as he came out of the glamoured cave.

"Let her go. She doesn't know anything that would be harmful to your pack," I tried again. It was too late; we were both in way too deep. The worse they'd do to me was return me to a fae. Of course, my experience with fae never ended well, and the last thing I wanted to do was be in their clutches.

"She knows about us. She knows about you. How can you even vouch for her? She'd betray you the second you gave her an inch."

"She wouldn't. Not all humans are like that. And she doesn't know enough even to tell," I spat as I struggled in the werewolf's hold. I was stronger than any human, probably even Forrest. But this wolf who held me was likely a trained Beta or enforcer. He was stronger, possibly the stronger of the two of them.

After using my powers and accidentally hitting Sixx, I was drained. I cringed as I recalled the bolt hitting her. She had been in so much pain. Closing my eyes, I tried to push away that shame for now. I knew it had been dangerous to call on that magic. It was wily and hazardous. But I had been pissed at how they were treating Sixx.

She couldn't see well, and worse, they were tossing her around. This had all been my fault. She shouldn't have been in this mess in the first place. Not to mention the fact that my aunt would be worried as hell when she got home and saw the mess left behind.

I'd worry about it later. Right now, I needed to think of a plan to get Sixx out of here. I could handle whatever these para psychos threw at me. But she was innocent and would pay dearly for my mistakes.

"The Alpha should be here soon. We need to make sure she is locked up, too."

"Should we take her to the other cave?" Stephen asked, watching me closely. The one holding me tightened his grip.

"No, it would be best to keep them together because if this one tries to use her magic again, she can watch as we torture her friend," the wolf holding me said as he dropped his lips to brush against the shell of my ear. I growled and yanked away from him.

"Fuckers."

The wolf pulled me back into the cavern. It was dark in here even for me, and my senses were stronger than a human. If I was having trouble, then Sixx probably couldn't see at all. I wanted to call out to see if she was doing okay, but I remained silent for now.

I huffed as the Beta holding my neck forced me forward to two manacles that were bolted to the wall with short chains. From what I could tell, they looked like they were made of iron. I wanted to shake my head at that. Iron didn't affect me like it did most other fae. Or at least, that's what my aunt and I learned about my para half.

There was so much we didn't know. Aunt Lola hadn't wanted to scare Sixx, but we didn't know for sure what the pack would do. I guess that they would eliminate anyone they saw as a threat. After I went back searching for the rogue, its throat had been torn out—no doubt the pack's handiwork.

The click of the cuffs broke the silence of the cave.

"You two idiots better not have brought me out here for no fucking reason," a voice boomed through the cavern. I flinched at the power in it. Usually, Alphas' powers didn't affect me. But I glanced over at Sixx where she was placed a little further back and on the other side of the cavern. The heavy weights of the iron cuffs balanced on the bones of my wrists. They both were just a little too tight, but at least they weren't scalding my flesh.

Sixx's head snapped up, and she curled a little closer to the wall. That fucker Stephen had torn her leg up, and I could smell the rusty, coppery scent of her blood. I clenched my fists tight as my power swelled up.

A vicious snarl snapped through the cave. It bounced off the walls as the heavy footsteps of the newcomer came further inside.

Double fuck.

The male who came in was massive and held himself with authority, which made me confident this was their Alpha. It surprised me that he didn't seem to know the whole story, so who were these two idiots? Anyone under his pack would have acted under his commands.

"Why do I smell a human and…" He paused, probably confused by my scent. Not the first time it happened and definitely wouldn't be the last. "A Halfling?"

"We followed the scents of the human that the rogue attacked and the scent of magic that surrounded it. Nicole also gave us a tip that a human in her school started to look up the Vycn."

I closed my eyes. That was not good.

I couldn't blame Sixx; she was scared and looking up information. Nicole should have kept her damned nose out of my business. If Forrest hadn't been sniffing around me, she probably would have. Fucking possessive she-wolves.

The day that Sixx helped me get out of being questioned by him, I realized that she was braver than most. I noticed a lot of the humans in the school, while they might have admired Forrest, also kept a safe distance from him and his group. Part of it had been human instinct to stay away, and I think part of it was that they generated that vibe about them.

It almost made me snort thinking of a tragically classic young adult novel. Shaking my head, I had to focus on the here and now.

An impatient growl came from the Alpha. He was massive, which didn't surprise me at all. Alphas usually were built like a linebacker on steroids. Forrest would probably end up as this pack's new Alpha when he was old enough or move on to create his pack. But as the male stepped closer, his gaze latched onto me.

"What is your other half?" His nostrils flared again. Many backwoods paras that lived outside of the cities in their little units could barely tell what I was. My magic was too diluted to know if I was a witch, fae, or a whole assortment of different magic users. But each year that passed, my powers grew.

It had been one of the bigger reasons we started to stick to smaller towns the older I got. That power increase, unfortunately, made the magic clearer to everyone in the school who was trying to figure out what the weird thing was about the new girl. And it caught me quite a bit of unwanted attention. Until I learned the best way to avoid it was to come into a new school and keep to myself.

"Now, why would I tell you that? It would make your job way too easy."

"And you are too young to be without a guardian. Eventually, they will come to seek you out. Then, I will have two paras to present to your elder."

That sent a shiver of fear down my spine. Aunt Lola would come looking for us, without a doubt. She could hold her own. I wasn't sure how she did it, how she had enough strength, but she did. It reminded me of when I had been about seven and displayed some powers at a local park. Unfortunately, we were living in cities at the time, easier to blend in. And a family of warlocks spotted me. They came in the night to discuss what they had seen with my aunt.

They recognized her as human and attacked. She moved with more strength and grace than a normal human being. But we never discussed it. We drove out after she managed to dispose of the ones who came by, and we never returned.

"Fae," I muttered, hating that I had to speak it out loud. I preferred to keep it quiet for a lot of different reasons. The first one was the way the Alpha was looking at me now. His eyes narrowed, and he grunted. One of the other two sparked a torch, and light bloomed over the room.

"Fucking Seelie, too," the Alpha growled through clenched teeth as he finally got a good look at me. I didn't know what that meant. I chose to ignore it for now and use the knowledge that I did have.

"No fae around. Guess you will have to take Sixx and me back home," I said with my most disarming smile. The Alpha was not amused.

"Unfortunately for you, I do know of an Unseelie a couple of towns over. I'm sure he will gladly come to pick you up and return you to the Veil where you belong."

I peeled back my lips.

"And what about the underage teenage girl you have locked up?"

My aunt always wanted us to stay away from paras because they thought only of themselves first. It was a dangerous world to live in but even worse when you were half-human. Half-weak in a society that prided itself on being strong. Something I was reminded of every day I lived.

I pushed away from the memories of my mother and how she passed. Right now, that anger would cloud my judgment and make it harder for Sixx and me to escape. I *would* get her out of this. She had tried to help me when she had no reason to.

And I believed she would have taken this secret to the grave, at the ripe, ripe age of 106 because she didn't seem like the type to go under so quickly.

"We will bring in the Blood Witch, but for now, you will both remain here. Her release will be much more swift than yours."

Fear pulsed through me. Blood Witches were unstable, their magic more explosive than mine. There were no guarantees. The Blood Witch would go in to erase the last couple of weeks but very well might take away all of her memories, everything that made her Sixx.

I lurched forward, unable to hold back my rage.

"No, just let her be! She doesn't know enough to hurt you. And she won't talk."

"I have lost too many of my wolves to human promises. I think not, little fae. The fact that I am allowing a Blood Witch to come in is a mercy because of her age. But if I find out that she has contacted any hunters, she is dead. And so are you. Truces be damned."

The Alpha turned away from us and strode out of the cavern, shoulders tense. Well, someone had been scorned in the past. I banked that for later. I needed to remember anything that I could to rile him up.

The werewolves gathered together at the mouth of the cave.

"Ana?"

"Yeah, Sixx?" I asked, keeping an ear on their conversation.

"Are we going to make it out of this alive?" she asked.

Chapter 13

Sixx

The fact that Ana remained quiet after I asked that did not bode well for us. It terrified me when the other werewolf showed up. He was *massive.* And everything in my body said to run for the hills. To get the hell out of here and away from that *man.* He wasn't scary looking, not from the bit of light shining from the torch they lit. Quite the opposite, but something about him told my instincts to run.

Ana bantered and tried to barter while I just listened in horror. My life was on the line. Still, I couldn't bring myself to speak. I couldn't bring myself even to pull away from the wall.

Ana remained strong, showing off her courage. But with my question still hanging between us, I wondered how much was bravado. Part of me, the part that wanted to continue to cower, said not to ask again. Just let it be.

"Ana?"

"I want to say yes, Sixx. But I don't know. I promise I'll do what I can to keep us alive," she said. But she couldn't do it alone. We both needed to be part of this. I figured the werewolves left their torch behind, and it was just the two of us. But I didn't want to assume.

"Are we safe to talk?"

"For now."

"If you hear them back in range, do you just want to say 'purple'?"

"Why purple?" Ana asked, a hint of amusement in her voice.

"It's easy to slip into a conversation without it making it obvious we are trying to hide something," I explained. Other words would have been too obvious that we were trying to clamp when they were near. But purple paired well with a lot of things and could be slipped in easily.

And as a bonus, it helped me center myself; it gave me something tangible to hold onto. We had a small plan that could lead to bigger ones. Because as scared as I was, listening to their plans, I didn't want to lose my memories. And I refused to lose my life.

"How is your leg doing?" Ana asked, looking at it. The bleeding had stopped. I still worried about being close to the dirty ground, but I could only keep it suspended for so long.

"A little better, I guess."

"If you were closer, I'd heal it for you. However, it takes a lot of magic for that. And while iron doesn't hurt, it does affect my abilities," Ana muttered.

"Are you finally going to reveal what you are to me?" I tried to joke even if my attention was split between so many different things. Maybe we could use this to our advantage.

Ana got strangely quiet. Her head dropped between her shoulders, looking weighed down.

"My mother was human. But she died when she gave birth to me. I guess she had always been on the frail side. Having a supercharged baby had been too much for her system. Especially since, according to Aunt Lola, she was still heartbroken over the male who left her behind.

"Aunt Lola never knew much about my father. I think my mother knew just about as much as she told Lola. But my mom had been missing for almost a year before she arrived back on Lola's doorstep, three months pregnant with me. From what we know, he was a fae. And not like a little, floating around, mischievous fairy. Like the tall, dark, and dangerous kind. They are rarely seen outside of their realm. And if the werewolves find a fae, they will probably force me back into their realm." Ana paused. "The Veil is a dangerous place. They don't follow the laws of our world.

And from the little information Aunt Lola and I have been able to gather, I never want to visit."

Ana looked at me, the frown on her face so deep-set I worried she would look like that forever. But the lines loosened.

"Aunt Lola became a determined woman, that is for sure. She took me in, even with all my complications, after my mother passed. She was heartbroken because they had lost their parents at an early age in a car accident. Lola, even though she was younger, had always been the responsible one. And sometimes I ..."

Ana got quiet. I moved over and tried to offer whatever support I could. We were in this together now. And hearing a bit about her life helped distract me.

"Yeah?"

"I hated my mother for what she did to Lola. I didn't know the woman, and I still have these moments of pure hatred for her. And I hate the male who offered up his sperm to make me. Neither one of them deserve a space in my mind."

I thought I had a hard time growing up, but the more I thought about it, the more I understood her point. Her aunt had to go through hell, losing the only family she had left for a year, only for her to return and then pass away. Not only that, but here I was wading into the pool of this world, and I was overwhelmed. How would a new mother with a daughter with superpowers even begin to handle all of this?

"My parents named me after the date and time I was born because they didn't want kids. The thought was not pleasant for them. I had been a surprise for them, Sixx, born on June the 6th at six a.m."

Ana was quiet for a moment before she laughed.

We spent the rest of the night, or what I assumed was the night, talking about our childhoods—swapping stories, giving each other peace from the reality around us. We avoided the scarier topics, ones I didn't want to ask about yet. Eventually, exhaustion took over, and I ended up curled on the hard ground, freezing but asleep.

****

Sleep during situations like this was a precarious thing. For a precious hour or two, my mind had shut off completely. It allowed a window of peace, but far too soon, the danger hovered at the fringes of my mind.

What would the Blood Witch do to me? What would they do with Ana? What would happen to me if things didn't work? Did I want it to work? Go back to everyday life after this?

The correct, concrete answer should be yes. What other option could there be? I was supposed to go to college. Major in something. Do the whole college experience. Move away from home, make long-lasting friends. Meet the love of my life. All those cheesy stereotypical things popular culture said about college.

But in truth, all of our experiences shaped and formed who we were.

"Sixx! Purple is my favorite color."

The thoughts threading through my mind vanished at Ana's warning. I jerked wide awake. My entire body ached, and a headache settled in the back of my head. My throat was dry, and even though food should be the last thing on my mind, my stomach cramped.

"Who is it?"

"Fucking idiots," Ana snarled as her gaze remained on the opening of the cave. And I understood what she meant. Stephen, along with Nicole, walked into the cave. The sunlight streamed in from the opening and small cracks here and there in the cavern. It afforded us a bit of light, but it was still hard for me to see.

"I can't believe these two are the ones that are causing such a rift in the pack. Especially her," Nicole growled. Her head tipped toward Ana.

Nicole strolled up and threw back her fist and swung it into Ana's gut. She barely reacted besides a soft grunt. I flinched in sympathy. I scooted backward as Stephen got close to me. He leaned down, his nostrils flaring as he scented me.

"Human smells like fear," he grumbled with contentment. He enjoyed the idea of my terror.

"Well, we have to be quick; my father will be back soon with that Witch. I don't know why I don't just kill her outright," Nicole said, her top lip curling back. "I've had to deal with this fucking human since first grade. I'm done with her."

My throat closed up as Stephen moved closer.

"What the hell did Sixx ever do for you hate her so much?" Ana spat in my defense.

"She was always there. She was acting unassuming. Forrest noticed her. The other pack males noticed her. They all had dark fantasies about fucking the nerd."

I almost laughed out loud at that one. Forrest and the other guys that hung around their group over the years *never* looked at me. Not once, not twice. That wasn't me being harsh on myself but the truth. I had only one boy look at me that way at school, and he moved away two years ago. He had been my first and last kiss. I didn't put myself out there. I wanted out of this place.

"I'll admit, I think a human would be a nice treat. Wonder how they would submit," Stephen grumbled, reaching out to grab my neck. I wrapped my hands around his wrist to hold him back. I tried to move away, but he snapped his other hand out, gripping my waist in a bruising hold.

"You're not going to fuck her here. Sorry, today is for torture only," Nicole said as she showed off wicked claws that she raked across Ana's abdomen. Ana didn't even scream, but she tried to kick out, knocking Nicole away.

"Oh yeah, that's right. My brother was saying that you preferred to keep the attention on you so we would leave Sixx be. Well, Five isn't as immune as you," Nicole said. She came over to me, jerking her chin, indicating that Stephen should leave.

I whimpered as I tried to get away from her, but the bolted chain kept me in place.

"Fucking human ruining everything," Nicole growled.

Then, she lunged forward, and her claws punctured my fragile human skin with ease. She curled her fingers up, ripping muscles, and blood poured from the wound she inflicted. I didn't realize the horrible screeching sound that echoed against the cavern walls had been me. Not until she pulled free with a twisted smile on her face.

"You need to calm down, Nicole. We weren't supposed to leave any traces of ourselves behind." Stephen snapped his teeth at her. She didn't seem to notice or care. Vengeance was in her eyes for whatever reason. But fur burst over her skin as her muscles expanded. My heart pounded in my chest as the scent of wet dog hit my nose.

She was shifting. Right. In. Front. Of. Me.

"Out!"

A voice snapped with so much authority that I wanted to do as they said as well.

Chapter 14

The Alpha stepped in, blocking the light from the outside world, pitching me back into darkness. Teeth snapped inches from my face, spit hitting my cheek and making me cringe a little closer to the wall. Nicole made a grumbling noise, but I heard her bones snapping back into place and the subtle hiss of hair retreating. I shuddered because *oh my, gross*.

Nicole still stood between the two of us as the Alpha took another step farther into the cave. The light flowed around him.

"Go home, daughter. You'll face the consequences of your actions when I return home."

It was strange to think that the father of one of my schoolmates was the man who would potentially destroy my life. Not to mention Ana's. How could he be okay with doing this to us? I couldn't wrap my head around it. It was unreal to me.

"We should kill them both and be done with this," Nicole snapped back, not backing down. A vicious growl ripped from the Alpha, and goosebumps prickled over my skin. My mind screamed, *Get away*. And it was hard to ignore the impulse even as I felt the cuff digging into my skin.

"This is my decision, child. Out!"

I cringed at the volume and the command. Nicole's outline ducked her head, rushing out of the cave. Like a dog with its tail between its legs. The thought almost made me want to laugh out loud, but I held back.

"You may enter, Witch."

The Witch moved forward. She hadn't been what I expected. Though honestly, I didn't spend a whole lot of time considering what a Blood Witch would look like. But it wasn't the woman who stepped forward. She was *much* shorter than the Alpha, maybe only hitting about mid-chest on him. Which is where I probably would hit, too, if not shorter.

But in her defense, the man was…massive.

The Witch came in farther, and it shocked me to see that she was rather plain. I thought I was average and blended in well. But she took it to a whole other level. Soft mousy brown hair that hung straight to her shoulders. A pair of matching brown eyes that seemed almost dulled. Was she even really with us?

She was slight but not insanely petite. What struck me as odd was her clothing choice. I guess my misconceptions had been that she would have come in looking the part. Instead, she walked in wearing sweatpants that looked like they were well-loved and a long-sleeved t-shirt; it was as if the werewolf had dragged her out of bed. Worse yet, she wore crocs. My eyes went wide at her footwear. *Really?*

As absurd as her clothing choice was, I couldn't help but try to get away from her, injured leg be damned. She seemed so unassuming, but the closer she got, the more my skin prickled with awareness. There was something not right about her. *Wrong*, my brain screamed.

"This is the human?" Her voice rang dull, lifeless, and terrifying.

"Yes, destroy her memories of anything that had to do with our world. Especially that one." He tipped his chin toward Ana.

"Leave her the hell alone!" Ana yanked on her chains, gaining their attention.

"Quiet, Halfling. You're the reason this is happening to her. You'll live with the guilt for the rest of your life," he snapped. Did I sense a bit of not quite guilt in his tone?

"I'm not doing this to her. You are. You could just trust that she wouldn't betray our secrets," Ana said. I wanted to croak an agreement, but the Witch that I had thought so unassuming before was still standing there, staring ahead.

She wasn't really looking in my direction, but I felt the weight of her gaze on me.

"Your pup injured her. I will charge more for the healing," she said.

"Fine. Now get it done. These are human parents we will be dealing with, and they will notice their child's absence," he said.

The Witch moved forward until she practically stood on top of me. A steady flow of words tumbled from her lips before hitting my ears and wrapping around my mind.

It felt like they were binding to me, etched into my brain. But worse, as her words hit me, they crept into my bloodstream like sharp needles. The pain started slow but quickly developed into something so much worse.

Screaming echoed around the cavern, both mine and someone else's. One was in agony; the other was pleading. Memories that had been long buried came rushing back. The time my parents went on a weeklong vacation, leaving me with my elderly grandmother—who needed more care than I did. Or the time I saw Ana moving something without actually touching it. The memories were years and years apart but sat next to each other as if they belonged together.

How did these two events tie together? I didn't know, but what I did know was they started to disintegrate. The pain of losing both memories at once made my vision blacken. It felt like my muscles were all being pulled taut in different directions. It felt like my brain seized up, and fire ignited in my veins.

I screamed until my throat became raw, and all I knew was the pain.

Memories were pulled from the dark reaches of my mind and tossed aside. Each one that remained haunted me until the next appeared. The burning on my shoulder didn't help.

"Stop, you're killing her!" another voice screamed, breaking through the haze of pain.

"Keep going. How many more memories?"

"Many, they have started to bleed into her long term."

"No! If you continue to do this, you will kill her!"

"Then, the human will die. If she is not strong enough to survive this, she would never make it in our world."

My head twisted and turned. A brief, peaceful moment when the pain wasn't stretching me thin. I whimpered, peeking my eyes open. It felt like months had passed if not years. Memories flittered through my head, making it harder to tell how long it had been. But the light had dimmed, making it harder to make out the faces next to me.

"Release her!" Ana screamed.

A bolt of pain raced up my spine. My back arched, and it felt like I was being snapped in half. Once the pain faded,

I was left panting; spit dribbled down the side of my mouth, and tears stung my eyes. I wanted to wipe both the tears and spit away. But I couldn't move.

"Sixx!"

My head hit the ground with a solid thud, and I whimpered out in pain. God, I wanted the pain to stop. *Just make it stop.*

I had lived a very sheltered life. Some people go through their entire lives without knowing the pain of being hit, beaten, or otherwise. I would have gladly gone through the rest of my life, never having to experience pain like this again.

Another scream caught my attention. My head lolled to the other side, away from the wall of the cave to Ana. Her arms lit up like the fourth of July; blue electric currents flared and sparked. They zapped and zipped. The smell of burning flesh hit my nose, and I gagged.

Ana screamed again, but this time, she yanked her arms forward, releasing herself from the bolts on the wall. The chains dangled, taking on her charge as she glared at the Alpha and the Blood Witch.

"Ana! Sixx!" Another new voice was added to the mix. I was too exhausted, too weak to move. I looked down, but all I could see were the Blood Witch's legs and the Alpha. The Alpha moved, roaring as he attacked.

"Aunt Lola!" Ana jumped into action and swung her electrically charged chains. She held them close enough to attack without losing control. The Alpha turned his attention back to her, knowing she was probably more of a threat. But the Blood Witch turned to face the showdown when Lola stepped into view. She looked like an avenging angel.

Like Angel, from the TV show, though. She was dressed in form-fitting leather that allowed her to move fluidly. Her muscles were toned, supple, and tight. Looking at her biceps could give guys a complex. But she swung a weapon around that had a long handle and a wicked curved blade at the end. It looked like a reaper's scythe. The Blood Witch jumped back for once, showing a bit of emotion, baring her teeth.

"Back off, human. I have no quarrels here. I will leave no harm to you or the others, and I have been paid a decent amount to forget it happened," the Blood Witch said, dropping her head in a nod. Lola watched her for a moment, her chest heaving. It might have been my imagination, but it looked like her arms shook.

"If you ever threaten my girls again, I will kill you," Lola said with clenched teeth.

"Understood, *stavka*," the Witch said with a bit of venom and respect in her tone. It was strange, but my head felt too fuzzy to analyze it.

Instead, it kept screaming, *We are saved, but not safe.* Ana still battled with the Alpha, who hadn't shifted into his wolf form, thankfully. As big as he was as a human, who knew how big he would be as a monster?

Ana whipped out her chains again. She was close enough she managed to loop it around his neck. I didn't get to see much after that since Lola stepped into my view and crouched down next to me, setting her weapon by my head. I wanted to move away from the blade, but my insides felt like jelly, and I didn't think any part of me was solid anymore.

"Sixx, can you hear me?"

I locked eyes with her. I indicated that I did with the smallest nudge of my head, but it sent another bolt of pain through me.

"Okay, good. I know you're hurting, but we've gotta go quickly. Okay? I have a friend who is coming up behind us to do a sweep. We need to be out of here before he arrives. I am going to lift you, but honey, I'm going to need your help."

I nodded weakly. If it meant getting out of this hell, then I would do whatever she asked. Whatever. She moved so that she stood behind me, helping me into a sitting position. I groaned as tears pricked at my eyes. It was painful to move. But as painful as it was, the idea of freedom from this place was all the incentive I needed to make me desperate enough to fight through it.

"Good job, Sixx. You're doing so well," Lola encouraged. She got me to stand, and I leaned against the cavern wall when she stooped to pick up her weapon. Ana and the Alpha had disappeared. Lola had her weapon in one hand and pulled me close, wrapping my arm around her shoulders.

"Come on, sweetie."

Chapter 15

The days that followed were kind of a blur. I remembered Lola getting me out of the cave and coming across two werewolves with their throats slit open. I gagged, and if I had any food or water in me, I would have most certainly thrown up. The violence wasn't something I was used to. But more than that, seeing a dead body, human or not, was a jarring sight.

Ana had managed to subdue but not kill the Alpha. She came out not looking so great herself. But Lola got us out before her *friend* arrived. At least, she kept calling him her friend and that we needed to be out as soon as possible. Ana didn't question her, so I didn't, either. Lola promised us both that the whole pack would get a visit and never recall that I knew their dirty little secret.

Because of my injuries and Ana's, we needed to stay out of the public eye. Their scent would remain until we were healed. Ana had a bit of healing magic available to her, but we were hesitant to use it because it drained her.

On the fourth night, the night before we had a smaller healing session, Ana was asleep in the room we were sharing. The first night, we tried sleeping in separate spaces, Ana in her room, me on the pull-out couch, but fear had driven me up to her room. There was a sense of safety in our numbers. But I woke up in the middle of the night thirsty.

I had gotten into the habit of bringing water with me to bed, but that night, I forgot. I crept down the stairs, trying not to wake Lola. She needed her rest.

As I stepped down into the living room, I noticed the front porch light was on. Lola was always pretty good about turning it off before we all went to bed. She didn't like to attract attention to the house. Fear spiked inside of me, and the desire to call for Ana hit me hard.

My stomach twisted, though, because I didn't want to have to call her for every little thing. I needed to learn to stand on my own two feet again. I stepped over to the window and peeked out. Lola sat on the small porch with a stout glass in her hand as she stared out into the night. My panic eased, and I turned my heel to leave when a figure broke from the tree line.

A tall ethereal man stepped out. He had stunning features and almost glowed under the moonlight. He looked Asian from where I stood, and the closer I got, the more I realized his features were of Asian heritage.

Lola leaned back in her chair, looking relaxed. She said something, but the glass between us muffled her words. Curiosity and a whole lot of paranoia piqued my interest. Crouching down so I sat under the window, I pulled it open just a crack.

"Taken care of?"

"Yes, and it is time for you to pay your end."

"Any way I could persuade you to wait just a little longer?" Lola asked. My brows bunched together. What did that mean?

"Not this time. You know the rules."

"Yeah, well, I just hadn't been expecting to cash in on my third charm quite yet."

"Yet here we are."

"Easy there, Xinwei. It almost sounds like you care," Lola said with a bit of light teasing in her voice. I peeked up to see the scene ahead of me. The man she spoke to, Xinwei, had short black hair slicked back. His tall frame was all muscles and dangerous. He had an air about him that made me want to run in the opposite direction. Definitely paranormal. I ducked back down.

"You are a foolish human, which I told you many times before. You shouldn't have made the deal."

"You accepted it."

There was a moment of silence. I twitched, wanting to move to look up through the window but worrying that one of them would see me.

"All right, let's do it," Lola said.

I gulped. Do what exactly? I didn't want to stay to find out. There was a lot about this world that I didn't know yet. Ana and Lola let me know everything that I needed to navigate this new world safely. But the information that they were telling me also scared me. It put me in a dangerous position.

I crept away from the window and crawled into the kitchen before I made a move to stand. I grabbed a bottle of water before returning upstairs, glancing back over at the window. Lola still sat outside, taking a long sip of her drink. Whether the para was still out there with her, I had no idea.

I realized this world was a very lonely existence for those who lived on the outskirts of it. Lola and Ana had each other. But other than that, they kept hidden from both sides. No humans got too close because what happened to me would happen to them. Or worse. And I had missing points in my memory. I reached up to touch my shoulder.

It was tender but scarred over. It would always be a reminder of the time we spent in that cave. I was weak enough to admit that sleeping in the pitch-black wouldn't be a thing for me for a very long time. But as I climbed the stairs back to the room I shared with Ana, I felt marginally better. I fell asleep, still thinking about the conversation that Lola had outside.

****

"Males. Females."

"Why not just man, woman?" I asked, still confused by this new terminology. Of course, in many of the books I read, they referred to paras and aliens. But the aliens made more sense to me since they weren't human, and it was a human term.

"I mean, even saying male, female might not be quite right. Some paras don't necessarily even have genders. But it's just how it is," Ana explained as we sat on the couch the next day. The more I thought about what I thought I saw downstairs, the more I realized it probably had been just a dream. I let it go, mostly since when we woke up, Lola had made us a huge breakfast.

Ana spoke out of the corner of her mouth, telling me that this was a rarity and that her food was excellent so don't ruin it for her. I stifled a laugh, which made both of them smile.

Ana and I ended up in the living room on the couch where we had been spending most of our time recovering after breakfast. Lola stepped into the room as I rolled my eyes at Ana.

"They don't like being compared to humans, either. Ana, would you mind if Sixx and I have a little chat?"

Ana looked over at me then back at her.

"Sure, but she is my best friend, Aunt Lola. You can't steal her away."

A half-hearted smile tugged at Lola's lips.

"Never."

Ana smiled.

"I mean, after all, I am too fucking cool for her to pick you over me."

"No, you have more sass than I do. I grew out of it. One day you will, too."

"I hope not," Ana said with a smile before heading upstairs to take a shower. I turned my attention to Lola, starting to suspect the dream wasn't a dream. Had she seen me? Was she going to explain what happened out here?

"There is something I wanted to discuss with you privately. Human to full human," Lola said, watching me closely.

"Okay?"

"This world you stumbled into, it's very dangerous and honestly not incredibly rewarding. There are pockets of happiness. But..." Lola paused to look up the stairs where her niece and adoptive daughter started the shower and proceeded to start singing loudly and terribly. "That's life, right, Sixx?"

I looked back at her. This time, I really looked at her. Her skin was pulled tight against her bones. Her pallor was a little paler than it should be. My stomach sank. Indeed, it only had to do with the stress of the last couple of days. She had been through a lot as well. She spent three days searching for two stolen teenagers, one she devoted her life to, the other a stranger. But over the last couple of days, I felt closer to them than I did my parents, which wracked me with guilt.

I called them as soon as I had been able to. I explained that I ended up staying with Ana, a new friend, that her guardian had been out of town and she felt uncomfortable staying home by herself. My parents bought the lie without needing any more information than that.

Lola called the school for both of us, posing as my mother, taking care of that obstacle.

"I have a favor to ask you," Lola said, pulling my attention back to her.

"Yes?"

"Will you take care of her? I know she seems so well put together. With a guardian like me, how could she not?"

I smiled with a bit of humor. This woman shaped Ana into the person that she had become. And I saw Lola in Ana the more I spent time with them. But her words sent a skitter of fear down my spine.

"Last night, you were speaking with a male, looked Asian, his name was…"

"Don't say his name," Lola snapped quickly, her gaze flickering from me to the door going upstairs. Her shoulders tensed then sagged. "I didn't know you heard us. How much did you hear?"

"Not a whole lot. But I can gather from this conversation and the one you two were having last night; you offered something in exchange for Ana and my freedom?"

Lola inhaled sharply through her nose and looked away from me, ashamed.

"Everything I have done in my life I have done for Ana. Trust me when I say that you don't need to worry yourself over what I discussed with that male last night. Forget his name. Forget it ever happened. And please, just…" Lola looked back at me with a plea in her eyes, in her voice, in everything she was. "Promise me you will take care of her."

"Shouldn't it be the other way around?" I asked.

Lola gave me a sad smile.

"The biggest difference between us and paras, and please remember this, Sixx, is that we are human. They are not. Ana straddles the line, and she needs a reminder every once in a while that she is human, too. She needs someone to ground her. To be with her."

It hung in the air between us.

When she is not here.

"Ana has become a dear friend. I don't think I could ever let her down. Not after all we have gone through," I said honestly. "But she needs you, too."

Lola gave me another sad smile.

"You girls are so young. You have so many adventures ahead of you. Let's not worry about that right now. Come Monday, you're returning to school. And thanks to my intervention, the pack will not remember either one of your involvement. So do not garner their attention again," she scolded kindly.

I cracked another smile. This home was filled with happiness and love. Affection and caring. It felt like I had finally found a home.

Epilogue

6 Months Later

The casket lowered into the ground, and my heartfelt heavy in my chest. Tears streamed down my cheeks. I couldn't stop them if I tried. Ana held tight to my hand. Her grief weighed her down, but she didn't show it as openly as I did. Not only had she lost both of her parents before she entered this world, but she also lost the only family she had left.

Lola's cancer hit hard and fast. It was already in the late stages five months ago after she saved us from the werewolves. I noticed her getting skinnier and weaker as the weeks went on. Ana, I thought, knew too, but she was scared to face it. I had been the one who ended up stepping up and insisting we were taking Lola to the doctor.

Lola didn't seem surprised by the news. She was resigned to the little time she had left with us. But she got to watch her niece graduate. We arranged for Ana to live with me; it started sooner than we expected. Lola had taken a horrible turn for the worse in this last month.

It pained me to think about her in that fashion. I preferred to think of her as the woman who bravely came into a werewolf's den to save us. That had been something we lucked out on as well. The pack forgot all about us. I had to learn to control my reactions around Nicole, though, and Ana helped with that.

But we were done with school now. We would figure out everything later.

After.

Ana's shoulders sagged, her hair sweeping down, curtaining her face. She clutched my hand a little tighter. I hated the pain that she was going through. I wanted to be able to shoulder her pain. But this was a pain that couldn't be shared. The best I could do was to live up to my promise to Lola.

I would be there for Ana.

I'd become her sidekick and her link to humanity.

To Be Continued In...

The Sidekick Chronicles:

Sixx and the Hellhound

LAST WORD FROM THE AUTHOR

Don't forget if you loved, meh, or just didn't much care for the book at all, that reviews are so important for authors, and please don't forget to leave one. Even one liners are helpful! There is much reviews can do: tell an author to keep working on a certain series, whether this genre is for them, gives them encouragement to do better.

Thank you all for your support.

Stuff about the Author

Becca Vincenza lives in wonderful Michigan. She has an obsession with candy, her animals, and of course books. When she's not wearing her author hat, she's working to pay off her student loans for her acquired English degree.

Contact with her:
Facebook:
https://www.facebook.com/beccavincenza
Facebook Group:
https://www.facebook.com/groups/926377960845819/
Website:
https://beccavincenzaauthor.wordpress.com/
Bookbub:
https://www.bookbub.com/authors/becca-vincenza
Tiktok:
https://www.tiktok.com/@beccavincenza?lang=en
Newsletter: https://bit.ly/2FhxJB8